OH! BALLS!

A NOVEL

GEORGE ONSTOT

ALSO BY GEORGE ONSTOT

Bullies on Juice
Macho Fellows
Hole in One
Entrepreneur
Tee & A
Native Grrl
Bum Love
What's Your Problem?
Ragin' Cajun
Life's a B*tch

1

She owned the first bare belly button I saw after arriving at the Masters. Fortunately, the rest of her was pretty hot, too. Sometimes, women who have big, ugly stomachs don't know they're unsightly—or don't care—and walk around with bare midriffs that turn *my* stomach.

A nice surprise, she was: a long-haired brunette in a pair of much-too-tight, really faded Levi's, looking very much like a college cheerleader. Her tummy was as tight and flat as a 12-year-old boy's ass, and her zoomers seemed desperate to burst out of her flimsy knit top. Around her neck hung the credentials to enter whichever hospitality tent she chose to honor with her presence.

She also had a clubhouse badge for the Masters.

"Beautiful woman," muttered Jake Grimsley. We gazed at her as she stood on the veranda. We were unsure if she knew we were checking her out, or if she knew we existed.

"I would love to take her picture," Jake added. "Would that be uncool?" He, like everyone else, owned a smart phone and could take high-resolution pictures of people wherever he went. But he knew it didn't mean he should just walk around taking pictures of people, or ask pretty women to pose with him.

"Very uncool," said Gil Donaldo.

"Go ask her anyway," I said. "Why not? The worst that could happen is she'd slap your face."

Usually the veranda was filled with rich old men in green jackets, countless other overprivileged people sitting at tables under umbrellas, businessmen in threes and fours putting intense pressure on themselves to sell their expensive goods and services to the affluent, greedy old men surrounding them, and media eggheads wandering around, trying to get someone to tell them something they could repeat to the people out there who wanted some gossip.

The businessmen interested me the most. They wore suits and shiny shoes that distinguished them from the green-jacketed rich guys who could afford to spend hours on the golf course and take it seriously. The men in suits, like the servers in white, were working-class Joes trying to sell equipment, or maybe they were the bosses of golf organizations. The youngest and most aggressive of the suits, the sports agents, kept looking around for the young men who showed the most promise and might be gullible enough to believe the agents' promises.

Wives of golf pros wandered into and out of the veranda. Some were pretty, others not. Those wives would have had their meals inside, while talking about chronic illnesses, underachieving children, aerobics classes not taken and UPS deliveries overdue.

My friends and I had entered the veranda by stepping over the velvet rope and nodding hello at the security guard whose job presumably was to make sure the Wal-Mart types stayed out. That was when we first saw the young lady with the luscious navel.

Clearly, that was her first time there. If she had been a whore looking to do some business with those moneyed old farts, too bad for her. Their shafts had lost their stiffness years earlier. All they wanted now was to find drivers that would give them more distance whenever they teed off.

"Grover," Jake Grimsley said to me, "it's a shame that she's the Prick's mother."

"She's nobody's mum," I said. "I had a mum. I've known lots of them. She's no one's mum. Not with that body."

Gil Donaldo said, "It's hard to believe, but she's Lorna, the Prick's mother. Jake's right."

I shook my head. "She's *Lance Priklan's* mother?"

I must have said it too loudly, because the security guard glowered at me.

I did some fast mental arithmetic. Lance Priklan was pushing twenty, the newest Next Big Thing in men's golf. We seemed to have one of those young hotshots altogether too often, and they usually faded away as fast as they came up. When they faded away, it was often because they were young, they got sick of golf and started to realize that there was plenty more good stuff in life.

The Prick was well over six feet, buffed out from weightlifting and handsome enough to be on the cover of *GQ*. He had an armload of amateur titles and enough product endorsements to keep him busy for a while. He could whack the ball a mile and make putts as well as anyone I'd ever met. His age meant that his mother must have been pushing forty, but she could have told me she was thirty-two and I wouldn't have called her a liar.

"Lance Priklan," I said, "is a big boy. I guess he got his size from whichever of his mum's boyfriends boffed her at the wrong time of the month."

"I doubt she had a bunch of boyfriends," said Jake. "A woman like her? She would be much too selective. The guy who fathered her son probably had a lot going for him, and he was the only one good enough to get in her pants."

"Could be you're right," I said. "Still, why I haven't I seen her before at these things? I would have remembered her."

Gil Donaldo said, "She's been at a few of these that you've missed. You haven't been to that many PGA events lately."

I nodded. "Yes. I was off doing other things. What was I doing?" I scratched my head. "Yeah, I was busy being kicked out of my house by my wife."

I thought for a minute about another sexy thing who had captivated my soul by wearing clothing that scarcely covered her marvelous curves. Simone Allerd had dressed that way because she was a barmaid, and her boss thought customers would drink more if the lady who served them had her zoomers spilling out of her top and jeans that almost didn't reach past her butt-crack and pubic hair. Simone got sick of her job soon enough and quit, and soon after that the owner was convicted of a bunch of crimes and did some serious time.

Just then a media star approached us—Clark Irving, sports columnist for the Boston *Globe*. I'd first become acquainted with him when he was another scrappy young reporter in Washington state, not long out of U. Dub's vaunted journalism school and dissatisfied with the modest job he'd ended up with. Clark had wanted to write a book with me, since I was the first professional golfer he had ever met. I had said, 'Yeah, sure, Clark, we'll do that,' and then he got a better job elsewhere. Our book didn't happen, and I couldn't have cared less. But in the years after that, he had become a hotshot columnist and a bestselling author.

Clark's first bestseller was *Boom Boxes: How Women's Basketball Pulled Some Black Beauties Out of the 'Hood*.

Someone had given me a promotional copy of that book and I'd read damn near the entire first chapter.

Since then, he had written a couple more bestsellers. I could probably remember their titles, if I tried hard enough. He always seemed to be publishing a new book.

At the Masters that day, Clark had on a faded golf shirt, old baggy shorts, sandals and a Seattle Mariners baseball cap, to show the others that he didn't give a shit about how he looked.

"Gentlemen," Clark said, "who's your pick for this year's Masters?"

"Tiger Woods," I said.

"Oh, that's too easy," Clark replied.

"Then Grover Bobbitt," I told him.

"That's the spirit!" Clark said. "Root for the underdog." He walked away, cackling.

I looked some more at the woman on the veranda. "I'll tell you something," I said to Jake and Gil. "There are groupies and sluts and hangers-on who dress her, letting it all hang out like that, but she's supposed to be a mature, sensible woman. What's the point she's trying to make?"

"Gee, Grover, I don't know," replied Jake. "Why don't you go over there and ask her?"

2

I had turned 40, and as her way of saying Happy Birthday, my wife, Helene, dragged me into divorce court. She became Mistake Number Three; Simone Allerd had been Mistake Number One, and Alicia Theodore Mistake Number Two. Simone, to quote Sheryl Crow, was my favorite mistake.

Helene demanded that I move out of our million-dollar house near West Shore, the one she demanded that I buy for us. She explained that I had been quite a douche bag for a husband, and what could she do about a man whose highest ambition in life was to win some golf contest in the States where they gave you a green jacket?

I found out I was soon going to be homeless and divorced when I arrived at our house and saw a sign on our front door: NO JEHOVAH'S WITNESSES OR FAILED GOLFERS WELCOME HERE.

Our big problem was that Helene by then had acquired socialite aspirations. She had concluded that being married to a professional golfer not named Tiger Woods was an unacceptable situation. By then she'd had some success of her own, hung out with other rich ladies in Bayporte, went shopping at the best stores and got their hair, fingernails and toenails done every fifteen minutes. Helene sometimes forgot that her socialite friends had been receptionists, clerks and food servers before meeting the rich guys they married.

I persuaded her to let me stay in the house I had bought until I could make other arrangements. Our cohabitation could have lasted much longer if I hadn't fucked up at one of her hoity-toity social evens. My missus had made me take a bath, then dressed me up and forced me to escort her to Bayporte Symphony Hall to listen to the orchestra play whatever the hell kind of classical music society folks pretended to like. Immediately afterwards, we went to the Bayporte Club to talk about shit that the snobs pretended to care about.

At home, Helene, enraged, said I had yawned, belched, farted and fallen asleep throughout an evening that I *knew* meant so much to her.

"You asked the conductor how much he got paid to wave his stick in the air like that. What was *that* all about? Grover, are you retarded?"

I shrugged. "Hey, I was just trying to make conversation. I mean, what can a person say to a conductor?"

She snarled at me. "You are a fucking sack of shit!"

"You're not sounding like such a highfalutin society lady right now," I told her. "You sound very much like Helene Macdonald, the girl I married. She was no better than I was. In many ways, she was a lot worse."

Awful!

I really didn't judge people by their wealth, neighborhoods or backgrounds. Well, maybe I did. Alicia Theodore had grown up in a West Shore mansion, and as time went on I found out she'd ridden the dick of every horny guy in Greater Bayporte before meeting me.

Helene, like so many other ME ME ME women, thought her good looks entitled her to a VIP pass through life. She'd been born into a modest family that lacked the means to buy her everything she wanted. God had made a mistake, and she needed to correct His error by marrying into an affluent family that could afford to give her that pass. The rich guy who put the ring on her finger didn't need to be handsome; he could be a paunchy, balding, swarthy Mediterranean bastard with a weird accent. *She* was beautiful enough for both of them.

Helene, like my other exes, started golfing, albeit for very different reasons. Simone and Alicia learned golf because they considered it fun and challenging Helene did it because Bayporte's elite people did it and she desperately sought their acceptance. So, despite her dreadful tee-offs and countless missed putts, she gradually became one of the more competent, and certainly the prettiest, lady golfer at my favorite local club, Placid Oaks.

If I had been much more intelligent, or at least much less naïve and oblivious to what was directly in front of my face, I would have observed what my wife was up to. Helene had regressed to her former self and was doing her old thing: luring away married men for quickies and destroying their families just because she could.

I knew perfectly well that she believed I was her consolation prize, and that if she had met some prosperous man who owned a yacht and his own jet, she would have fallen in love with him immediately and left me forever without a moment's remorse.

'Finally,' she'd have said to herself, 'I've gotten my VIP pass!'

To me she said, "After our divorce is final, I want the house and the Mercedes."

"OK. I don't want the Mercedes, anyway. Too much of his dried come is on the back seat."

"Fuck *you*, Grover!"

I had gotten her all upset. I felt good. I smiled as I went away.

I ended up moving into an apartment near Northup University. I should have enjoyed it—I had attended the U. years earlier and always enjoyed being around young women. Plus, I was single now and could try to seduce them. But I was alone and *lonely*, and being near the college just reminded me of how old I had gotten and how young the students remained. Also, I had enjoyed Helene much of the time, especially when she wasn't cussing me out or spending all my money. But as time went on, I got used to having no wife, and my status became quite a good thing once I realized there were Lorna Priklans in the world.

3

So far as golf went, being divorced and lonely was a trivial matter compared to turning forty.

Most people are probably unaware of how old 40 is for a golfer, particularly one with two decades of experience yet has *never* won a major tournament. By majors, of course, I mean the Masters, US Open, PGA or even the Bayporte Open. I'd been there, done them but never won.

Listen: Winning a major is the only way a professional golfer can look into the mirror and say to the man looking back at him, "You have succeeded in life." Without that validation, he can be healthy and handsome and a delight to his friends, but in the mirror he will always say, "You're a fuckin' loser, guy."

But once the golfer wins the major, the world falls in love with him and he becomes *The Man*—at least for 15 minutes—and for the rest of his life, even if his golf game sucks, he'll know, in his soul, that it was all worth it.

While I haven't check out this matter in Las Vegas, I would guess that the odds of a man 40 or over copping a win at one of the majors are about the same as his getting a steak at a vegan restaurant.

Truth is, over the years, countless men have gone out to play and called themselves professional golfers. Of that number, maybe half a dozen have won a major tournament at age 40 or older.

"Half a dozen men have done it," I'd said to my friends Jake Grimsley and Gil Donaldo any number of times since my 40th birthday the month before. They probably had gotten sick of listening to me, but too bad for them.

"Nicklaus did it while the Vietnam War was on," I reminded them.

"So you've said," replied Gil.

"Hale Irwin did it, too."

"You've said that, too," said Jake.

I ignored them. "If those two can do it, why can't I?"

"Because," said Gil, "you're not Nicklaus or Irwin. You're Grover Bobbitt."

"Fuck you very much," I retorted.

Jake and Gil cared about Tiger Woods, Steve Stricker, Jason Day and Phil Mickelson.

"I've thought about Nicklaus when he shot a sixty-five on the back half. He was—how old? Forty-six? And I've almost cried, because I've played the same course as a much younger man and shot a seventy-nine!"

"Seventy-nine on the last nine of the Masters?" Jake said. "That and ten dollars will get you lunch at McDonald's."

"As great as Nicklaus played that day, he beat Greg Norman and Tom Kite by this much." I held out two fingers spaced an inch apart.

"It's a tough game, Grover," Gil said. "Nobody has ever claimed otherwise."

"Hale Irwin? He was forty-five when he won his third Open at Medinah. He sank a huge putt and danced around. When I played Medinah, my eye-hand coordination went on vacation and I finished, like, tied for last place."

"Tied for last is no fun," said Gil.

"When Boros won in New Mexico, it was so hot and humid that some people couldn't stand it. He beat Arnold Palmer by one stroke."

"I'll bet Palmer *had* a stroke over losing that one," Gil said, chuckling.

"Harry Vardon and Lee Trevino won majors after forty," I went on. "Why can't I?"

"Because you suck!" Jake and Gil said at the same time.

4

I believe that all opening lines sound alike, so the guy speaking them may as well be saying, "Hello, young lady. I am a doofus. Please reject me." So Jake, Gil and I entered the veranda and they hung back while I hit on her.

"Buy you a drink?" I asked her.

She pointed to her half-full glass of white wine. "Got one already."

"Want another one?"

"I'll buy my own, thanks."

I sighed and said, "So…"

"You're wasting your time. I'm not interested. Please go away." She turned her attention to her glass of wine.

"But I haven't finished charming you yet."

"You haven't started."

I nodded, so that my friends would think she hadn't yet told me to fuck off. Looking down and around, I felt pleased to see that she had no jewelry in her navel, nose or nipples and probably had none in her clit, either. I wondered about her zoomers, and why a woman her age thought it was OK to walk around braless (plus, she was rocking those low-cut jeans that barely covered her junk).

"Do you see those two guys over there?" I nodded to my right.

She looked in that general direction. "What about them?"

"They're both wearing green jackets."

She nodded. "That's because they've both won the Masters."

"Yes. Exactly. I want one, too. It's kind of the thing that I want most in the world."

She paused. "Well, you could go to a men's store and buy one and wear it here. Maybe no one would know the difference."

"Oh, I think they would know the difference."

"Of course, your other option would be to win this Masters and they would give you a *real* green jacket."

"Easier said than done," I told her.

This lady had a brain. I liked that. Many guys didn't. The guys who liked dumb women knew that dumb women let their guys boss them around. In my world, most of the women liked to talk about home improvements, offspring and relationships. That book about men being from Mars and women from Venus? It pretty much summed up things for me.

"Your outfit," I said, "is ideal for today. Hot and humid."

"That's why I wore it. Keeps me comfy."

"Not altogether appropriate for this milieu, though," I said.

"Am I baring too much? You're the first person who's complained."

"No complaints here," I said, raising my hands. "It's just that the weather here is unpredictable. Today hot and humid, tomorrow cooler and rainy. A person needs to know about these things."

"Fascinating," she said, nodding. "I'm talking to a weather man. All the while, I thought you were just Grover Bobbitt."

5

I must admit to being flattered whenever people recognize me. Surprised and flattered, especially when I'm twentieth or lower on the board. One of the *shmucks* still without anything to brag about. The kind of guy Tiger Woods would laugh at, if Tiger knew I existed.

"I know who you are. I follow golf," the beautiful woman said. "I'm Lorna Priklan."

She extended her hand. I shook it.

"Are you a member?" she asked me.

"Been one for the longest time. Occasionally I think I own this place. Then I see the guys in green jackets and that puts me in my place."

"Have you seen Lance Priklan play? He's my son."

The Prick.

"My friends and I thought you were his sister."

"He doesn't have a sister. Sorry to disappoint you."

"Oh, I'm not disappointed."

"What do you think of his golfing so far? I mean, does he have much of a future as a pro?"

Are you kidding?

"I've seen him on TV and on the practice tee this week," I told her. "He seems to have plenty of potential. Terrific swing, great motion, and he's as strong as an elephant. He can really hit that ball. If you have all that, you have a lot."

"Nice to hear," she said.

"Why don't you and I sit somewhere and talk some

more?" I asked her, my heart pounding.

"Let's."

We maneuvered through the other people on the veranda and went inside.

"I'm going to guess," I said, "that there's no Mister Priklan here or elsewhere."

"Good guess," she replied.

I had lived long enough, and been married enough times, to know that a woman with a beautiful body didn't walk around with her goodies on display if she had a husband or boyfriend. If there was a man in her life, he would damn sure travel with her, if only to make sure other men didn't grab at his woman's goodies.

"Separated or divorced?" I asked.

"The latter."

"His idea or yours?"

"Mostly his."

"He was a fool," I said. "Where is that doofus now?"

"Back in Santa Barbara, with the dewy eyed dollop of womanhood he left me for."

"That young, eh?"

She nodded. "I think it's in the back of his mind, or in the front of it, to start another family."

"So now you're divorced and homeless?"

"No, we have a house in Pebble Beach. That's mine now."

I frowned. "Pebble Beach is much too old for you. Or you're too young for it."

"Have you been there?"

"I'm a professional golfer. Of *course* I've been there. I've been humiliated by some of the world's greatest golfers there."

"I guess that's why you're so humble and modest."

"Do you consider humility and modesty attractive qualities in a man?" I asked.

She ignored this. "Bruce and I grew up in Woodside and went to Stanford."

"Cardinals, eh? Wow!"

She smiled. "Yes, I was Lorna Jean Hawes, Cardinals cheerleader."

"Sounds like *such* an all-American girl. Did you compete in the beauty contests?"

"No, I couldn't sing or play a musical instrument. Actually, I *could*, but not nearly well enough, and in those beauty contests, they place *lots* of importance on the talent aspect. It's not just having tits and ass and filling out a swimsuit." Then, "I did the cheerleader thing very well. I'm proud of that. Highly prestigious and *too* much fun."

"And what about Bruce Priklan?"

"He played football. Running back, good but not great. We went to the Rose Bowl and beat Michigan. Probably the best day in my whole life until Lance won his first amateur tournament. He gets his height and build from his dad, though Bruce has never had shoulders like Lance's." Lorna giggled. "I hope my son isn't juicing up. I think steroids are poison.

"Anyway, after graduation, Bruce took over his father's chain of auto-detailing stores and I got pregnant. Bruce was very much unprepared for parenthood, and very unsure that he wanted *me*, period. But he was a good sport about it. He was generous with his money—he bought me most of the stuff I wanted. I don't have to work, but I do it because I like it. My old friend and I have a little art gallery in Carmel. Her name is Katie Sanford. Her husband left her for her golf partner. How's that for decadence, California-style?"

She added that the women of those really exclusive California communities had only one aspiration in life—to spend money.

"Years ago," I said, "a friend of mine married a woman from Pebble Beach, La Costa, or wherever it was, and he told me that when those ladies got to talking about a server in some restaurant, they're referring to a restaurant in Marseilles."

Lorna laughed. "Those ladies are the ones who buy my paintings."

"Must be nice to live that way," I muttered.

"You know, I taught Lance to golf while he was still a little kid. He grew up in Pebble Beach, learning to drive and putt. I wanted him out there, doing that. Otherwise, I was afraid he'd turn out to be a beach zombie or a cannabis cultivator. You wouldn't believe how many people I know who are doing that. Bruce and I spent so many years going around to those tournaments. We both thought it was fun, too—until he met what's-her-name."

"What *is* her name?" I asked. "I'll bet it's Candy."

"Tammy."

I smirked. "That's almost as bad as Candy."

"Your wife, Grover Bobbitt." She paused, changing the subject. "She must have stayed home this week. And please don't tell me that you're a grieving new widower who's looking for some solace in his time of need."

"I'm going through divorce number three. That's how come I've learned to relate to women so well."

"Tell me—were all your wives bitches?"

I shrugged. "One of them is a decent human being. She deserved a better husband than I was."

"But the other two were bitches, right?" she asked.

"Well, they went crazy with my credit cards, and when they maxed out my cards, they looked for men with bigger lines of credit. My most recent ex, Helene, felt very disappointed that I didn't qualify for an American Express black card. She divorced me so she could find a man who liked dinner parties more than I did."

"Oh, was Helene a high-society type?"

"A high-society wannabe."

"Is she making much progress?"

"She still needs to learn that farting at the dinner table is a no-no."

"Yea, she'll have to work on that."

I sat back a bit and said, "Lorna, all nonsense aside, I'm just a lonely divorced guy. I'm at the Peachtree Inn and have no plans except eating, sleeping and golfing."

"We have something in common," Lorna said, smiling. "I'm staying at the Peachtree, too."

"I guess our meeting was meant to happen," I said.

Just then, Jake and Gil appeared at our table, looking down on us as we sat.

"We're going over to hit some balls," Jake said.

"I'll meet you there," I replied. "Tell Everett if you see him."

Everett Moore, my caddy, had been with me for close to a decade. Many people thought he looked and sounded a great deal like Eddie Murphy, and when asked if he *was* Eddie Murphy, he felt tempted to say yes, even though it would be hard to explain why Eddie Murphy was carrying some white guy's golf clubs. Everett probably envied, or resented, Eddie because Eddie had a much better lot in life. The two men shared similar looks and voices, and identical initials, too, but not much else.

"Lorna," I said, "do you know my friends Jake and Gil?"

The three exchanged greetings.

"Jake, you played well last week, at Bay Hill," Lorna said. "You were in the party ahead of Lance."

"I didn't see you there. Otherwise I'd have worn some Right Guard."

Lorna giggled.

"Aren't you cold?" Gil asked her.

"Excuse me?"

"You've almost nothing on. I'm afraid you'll catch the flu."

"Don't mind Gil," I said. "He makes breathtakingly inappropriate remarks all the time. He was born that way."

Jake said, "Lorna, I've hit practice balls with Lance. He's the strongest man I've ever met. He's accurate, too."

"He does his best." Lorna grinned.

Gil said, "Yeah, Lance is long. John C. Holmes wasn't that long—"

"Enough said," I told him.

Lorna and I looked around, to see if anyone was glowering at us. But no; these people didn't know about porn stars and their penises, and their conversations were about the tees, trees and flowers outside.

"Let's go," Jake said to Gil. "These two obviously don't appreciate just how charming we are. Plus, I have to whiz in major ways."

Lorna rolled her eyes and blushed.

Gil said, "Grover, you gonna meet up with us for dinner?"

"Maybe." I looked at Lorna. "Unless I get a better offer."

They went away, and Lorna leaned in towards me.

"I want to ask you a question, and I want an honest answer."

I shrugged. "Ask."

"Are you embarrassed by the way I look right now? By the clothes I'm wearing? No bra, flimsy top, low-cut jeans. Embarrassed?"

"I wouldn't say that. Should I be? Am I blushing and squirming?"

She nodded. "Yes, you're embarrassed because I am *so* underdressed for this place."

"Why did you dress that like today?"

She shrugged. "It was so hot and humid. I wore what was comfortable. It didn't occur to me that I was showing too much skin until your friend asked me if I was cold." She paused. "It's like going to the beach and I'm wearing a bikini, or topless, or nude."

"But this is a country club full of conservative, prudish old rich people who think everyone should be all covered up at all times. I am not embarrassed by your outfit, mainly because you are beautiful. Gorgeous face, perfect curves. What I would find offensive is a homely woman wearing an outfit that says to the world, 'See how fat and pimply I am? I don't like myself enough to try looking my best!'"

She frowned and hugged herself. "Now I want to swipe some old guy's green jacket and cover myself up."

I smiled. "I wish I had one to put on you."

She smiled back. "Every dog has his day."

We talked some more, mostly about Lance and golf. She told me of their deep disappointment over his need to miss his first Masters due to pneumonia.

"Let's get a drink later on," she said. "At the

Peachtree Inn."

"Only if you put on a bra and some undies."

She chuckled. "I'll wear something modest yet sophisticated."

I nodded. "It's crucial to dress prudently because if you go to a bar down here with your zoomers and butt-crack visible, the local yokels will start getting horny and they'll hit on you. Then I'll have to tell 'em to back off and they'll say, 'Make me, fucker.'"

She giggled. "I love it when a man defends my honor."

"Well, that's the problem. I'm too much of a wimp to defend anyone's honor, even my own. Those horny boys would kick my ass."

"I'll dress tonight in a smart black outfit so you can be proud of me."

"Nice," I said.

She smiled and added, "I've got a big week coming up. I'm going to watch Lance play golf, and I'm going to get together with the other women who are coming here to protest the males-only membership policy here."

"What?" I asked, feeling as if I'd just been slapped in the face and kicked in the stomach.

6

I called Gil and Jake and told them to eat without me. Then I called Lorna and told her to have her drink without me. What was up with that feminist-protest nonsense she was into?

I could have told them, "I wouldn't be any fun tonight." Instead, I said my back was acting up, which wasn't entirely a lie—my back always acts up. I could have added, "My hemorrhoids are as big as walnuts." I wanted to make sure I didn't scare off Lorna with my medical grievances.

I told her, "I'll get by on a room-service sandwich tonight and watch some pay-per-view porn."

"Whatever turns you on," she replied. "I'm tired, too. Let's have dinner tomorrow night. I'll dress up. Break a leg on the Par-3 tomorrow."

Click.

The thing I needed as a golfer was to hit the ball shorter distances with greater accuracy.

The following morning, Jake and I played together, and throughout the par-three, we got our balls to go everywhere but into a cup. We really, totally crapped out.

Why, I wondered, did all those people show up to watch the Par-3? To me, the Par-3 is just *such* bullshit. Of course, it's the one event where the fans can get physically close to the world's premier golfers.

Those fans crowd around every tee and green, and they get close enough to those elite golfers to hear them belch and fart. It's as if they're rock-music fans who have front-row-center tickets and can say, "I heard Bruce say this to Patti," or "Bono said some shit to the Edge between songs." The fan hears his music or golf idols say real things.

Fortunately, many of those people exist; if they didn't, I'd have lost my career (if one may call it that) years ago.

I felt tempted to blow off Lorna for dinner again. But I thought about it a bit and said to myself, 'Oh, go ahead and break bread with her. Maybe you can persuade her to call off the feminist dogs.'

If that didn't work, I could still have an enjoyable evening with her. Lorna was the kind to tap on her iPad for two hours at a time, reading all the news services. She could tell me about the day's events and issues. I had stopped paying attention to the military-industrial complex propaganda years earlier. Plus, I just wasn't interested in learning more about the weirdo radicals who hated us Westerners because we liked cheeseburgers, beer, soap, girlie magazines and women who didn't smell like stray dogs.

I might say, "Lorna, we should retire all those ridiculous university professors who preach 'diversification' and 'globalization..' Those clowns want to provide free college educations for illegals and they think the losers on death row should get satellite TV while the executioner waits for the lethal-injection drugs to arrive. What the hell you think of *that*?"

I honestly looked forward to saying all that to Lorna as we sat in the restaurant. I wanted to know how she felt about boring, conservative men like me.

7

The Peachtree Inn is located in a quaint part of Augusta, halfway between downtown and the Augusta National. The neighborhood is full of huge estates that are difficult to find because they're hidden on side streets. Most American towns have Augustas of their own—magnificent homes built by Coca-Cola, Levi's, Corn Flakes or other fortunes. Those houses, often three or four stories tall, are long on lawns, trees, gardens, history and charm, and short of closets and bathrooms. The Peachtree had been such a home, converted into a hotel and modernized in all the expected ways. I went into the bar alone, to pissed off about my golf pairing. They had posted the pairings earlier that day. I would be busy for the next couple of days. Naturally, I wanted to be paired with Tiger Woods, Phil Mickelson or any of the other famous golfers, but that didn't happen. What I got was a nine-AM tee time with a golfer even more obscure than myself. Guy Norman was his name. A guy named Guy. I didn't like that; was his sister named Girl? I once knew a lady named Niece; out of necessity, she had a fine sense of humor. If my parents had done that to *me*—named me Nephew—I would have marched down to city hall and traded in my moniker for a new one. Of course, my folks named me Grover, so I guess that's no improvement on Guy.

I had no chance of getting a quiet drink at the Peachtree Inn during Masters week. People came up to me, recognized me, said hidy.

"Grover Bobbitt?"

I nodded. "That's me."

"I'm Billy Joe MacDonald and this is Robby Ray Riggs."

"Damn glad to meet you." My mum had always told me: It doesn't cost anything to be polite. Especially in my line of work, where courtesy is expected and surliness seldom forgotten.

Billy Joe shrugged. "Aw, Grover, you know what the problem is right now? There just ain't enough whup around at the moment." He looked away and shouted, "Barkeep! A drink for Grover! Put it on my tab!"

I ordered a double Canadian Comfort over ice, since Billy Joe was paying for it.

He gave a nervous little laugh. "Hell, Grover, I didn't know you drank that *premium* shit."

"Ben Hogan had a few whenever he was playing," I said. "It helped him relax and fall asleep."

"Who's Ben Hogan?" asked Robby Ray Riggs.

"Just a guy I admired," I said.

Billy Joe and Robby Ray, tall and muscular, were far more presentable and personable than their names would suggest. Both wore golf shirts and pressed slacks. Their casual shoes looked immaculate. Both men had plenty of hair and white, straight teeth.

"We're damn glad to meet *you*, Grover, especially since we know you came all the way from Canada just to play golf here. We're from Atlanta."

"Damn fine city," I lied. To me, Atlanta was mostly endless distance, surreal traffic jams, drugs and killings and insufferable humidity. But I didn't say that to these two guys who could turn my teeth upside down.

"We played eighteen holes today," Billy Jo said.

"How'd you do?" I asked.

"I would've shredded that sumbitch except that I couldn't get a putt to go in no matter what," he said. "Do I speak the truth, Robby Ray?"

"He exaggerates," Robby Ray said to me. "He played decent golf today. But if he doesn't do better than Tiger Woods, he's like, 'I played shitty today.'"

Billy Joe chuckled. "Don't mind him, Grover. He thinks he's a funny bastard, always cracking jokes. I'm always saying, 'Don't quit your day job, Robby Ray, 'cause you ain't that fuckin' funny.'"

"We play a lot of golf in Atlanta," said Robby Ray. "Billy Joe's daddy owns a course. All greens, no houses. Beautiful place—no fairies, Jews or coloreds allowed, thank you very much."

"Is that right, Billy Joe?" I asked.

Billy Joe nodded. "We could host the National Amateur up there just fine, but they would never let us have it because of our 'no fags, Jews or blacks' policy."

"Then why don't you alter your policy and make it more tolerant and accepting?" I asked.

He frowned. "Why would we do that?"

I shrugged. "Just a thought."

"Hey!" Robby Ray said. "Grover, I need to ask you a question. Me and Billy Joe have been talking about a course we've heard about, but we're not sure where it is, and we're too lazy to look it up online. He says it's in Michigan and I say it's in New Hampshire."

"Well, what's the name of it?"

"Placid Oaks."

I guffawed. "You're both wrong. It's in Bayporte, Great Elizabeth, Canada. I was born and raised there."

"So you've played it?" Robby Ray asked.

"Many times. Great course."

"Yeah," said Billy Joe, "Tiger's talked about it on TV. Says he goes there to play whenever he can."

"Some dandy asshole," said Robby Ray, "came in here a little while ago, sayin' that Placid Oaks was the best course in the world and he pitied the fool who didn't have the sense to go there."

"If you ask me," I told them, "Placid Oaks is the best course in North America."

"For real?" Billy Jo scowled. "Even better than Augusta and Pebble Beach? That's horseshit. I don't believe a word of it."

"Don't speak to him that way," said Robby Ray. "After all, Grover's on the Tour. He's played all over the place, you know."

"He can play with your daddy's junk. He's full of shit if he thinks Placid Oaks is better than Augusta or Pebble Beach," retorted Billy Jo.

"Ouch," I said. Then, "Look, boys, I think Augusta is terrific. It has some of the best greens in the world. So does Pebble Beach. I'm not saying they're less than first-class courses. I'm just saying that, in my mind, all things considered, Placid Oaks is the best course on the continent. No disrespect meant to anyone or anything."

"That settles it," said Billy Jo. "We got to figure out where Canada is. Then we'll go there and play that sumbitch."

"Not so fast," I said. "You have to know somebody first."

"Aw, shit." Billy Jo glowered, as if he wouldn't mind putting a gun to my head and a Placid Oaks membership application in my hands, so that either my signature or my brain matter would end up on the document.

Then he said, "Don't mean shit. My daddy will call people and write checks. He'll get us in to play there."

Robby Ray said, "Grover, how about that cunt who's organizing a protest? What the hell you think of that?"

He meant Marni Sandusky, the muckraker who hopped from cause to cause. Even *I* knew about her, and I'd made a point of remaining ignorant of the Marni Sanduskys of the world. She headed a group called something like Women Who Have No Use for Men.

"They've given her too publicity," I said to the guys. "She's in love with the sound of her own voice."

"I think she has, like, half a dozen doctor degrees," said Robby Ray. "She thinks she's smarter than the average genius. I think she's full of shit. Maybe I'll tell her so when she gets here. She says she's bringing a thousand women with her."

Billy Jo smirked. "I hope they're cute. Those women wouldn't be so angry if they had a nice stiff one in them once in a while."

"Marni Sandusky is ugly," said Robby Ray.

"Put a paper bag over her head and you won't mind her ugliness so much," Billy Jo said.

"Oh, *my*." Robby Ray straightened up and raised his eyebrows. He looked past me.

"That's what *I* want for Christmas," Billy Jo said, turning around and looking in the same direction as Robby Ray. "No wrapping, no bow, just put it under the tree and I'll know it's for me. I'll never ask for anything else."

I looked where they were looking and saw her. Lorna. All covered up in stylish, well-tailored black material, face tanned and smiling, big eyes sparkling.

"My six-o'clock appointment is here," I said, taking Lorna's arm and walking her to our table.

8

I drank a Canadian Comfort over ice, then had another one.

"When I told you about my protest, you said, '*What?*' and I'm not sure I liked the sound of that," Lorna told me. "My protest is a serious business to me, and you need to respect that."

"Men have fought and died in two world wars so that you and your protest should be respected," I told her.

"I want you to take me and my goals seriously." Then she looked up and smiled. "Oh, here's Lance. He wanted to come by and say hi."

I stood; we both smiled and shook hands. Lance Priklan was who I would have been at twenty if God had liked me more. His dimples were deep and dark, smile blinding, blue eyes incandescent. His black hair was fluffy and messy in all the right places.

"I've on my way to meet two of my boys for beer and pizza," Lance told us.

"You're underage," I said. "Better have Coke."

"We'll have beer. They never card us."

"What do you think of Augusta?" I asked him.

He shrugged his prodigious shoulders. "It's all good. If anything, it could be harder."

"Harder?"

"Yeah. Where are the trees and sand traps? I want a course that makes me sweat a little bit."

"Oh."

"Maybe I'm just underestimating it, but it just looks too easy."

I nodded. "It's harder than you think. Plenty of challenges out there."

"Sure, if you don't hit the ball far enough, you're in trouble. But that's never happened to me." Then, "Are you on the seniors' tour now?"

His mum chuckled.

"Not yet," I said. "Maybe later."

Lance nodded. "OK. Good luck to you. I have to go. Catch you later, Mom."

"Get some rest, Lance. Winning the Masters won't be quite as easy as you think."

"I hear ya."

And he was gone.

"Does he have his own apartment, or does he just live in hotel rooms?" I asked Lorna.

She stuck out her chin, as if I'd just asked her, *Does Lance still make pee-pee in his bed?* "Of course he has his own place. He owns a house in Florida. He moved there for tax reasons."

I smirked. "He's not yet old enough to have a beer legally, but he owns a house in Florida for tax purposes. I wish I had *his* problems."

"He owns a three-bedroom house not far from Orlando. He plays golf there almost every day. He's played with Tiger and most of the other greats." She sighed. "Maybe he should have a nickname."

He already has one, sweetie. They call him The Prick.

Of course, I didn't tell Lorna that her son came across to me as being a shoo-in for the Smug Asshole Award. But Lance at twenty had already become a world-class golfer, and for that I gave him my grudging respect. Most people his age impressed me as being idiots, because their music, movies and video games had made them that way. They had the attention spans of fleas. At least Lance had the discipline and ambition to build himself up physically and learn to play a sport remarkably well. It's such a shame that today's young people can hear rap music's mindlessness but have never heard Diana Krall play "Walk on by."

"Lance," Lorna was saying, "seems very self-assured, but he's really not. His favorite place in the world is the golf course, where he really feels he has control over his environment. To him, it's like being in a movie—everything is possible. There are no limits."

"There seem to be no limits for him as far as golf goes. Who manages his money?"

"Bruce, his father. IAM—International Athletics Management?—met with Lance and Bruce and made a pretty persuasive pitch for handling him. But Bruce said afterwards, 'I can do a better job than those assholes.' So he became his son's agent and manager. He's negotiated Lance's deals with Apple, Versace, Bugatti, Patek Philippe and a few others. Bruce now has his own agency and wants more clients."

I said, "Bruce is smart to manage Lance. Let Dad shake him down. What's Dad's commission? Twenty percent?"

"Thirty. The same amount that IAM wanted."

I nodded. "Well, I guess Bruce has overhead to worry about."

Lorna smirked. "Lance's financial set up is just perfect. That stuff you've read in the golf magazines? It's all true."

"I'm illiterate. Tell me what the golf magazines say."

"They said that Lance was guaranteed ten million dollars a year even if he missed every cut."

I blew out a big breath. "I wonder if Bruce is hard-up enough for clients to take me on. Of course, I don't have Lance's armload of amateur trophies. In fact, I have one hundred percent of nothing as far as trophies go, and Lance has just about all of them. Right?"

She nodded. "National Amateur, two Westerns and an NCAA."

"Did he go to Stanford, too?"

"Yes, for one year."

I shook my head. "Poor boy. He'll regret dropping out...not."

We both laughed.

"You know, Grover, I'm regretting the fact that *he's* missing all that fun at Stanford. It's such a special place. I often miss all the fun *I* had there, too."

"I've heard it said, 'There are many fine colleges in California, but only one is named Stanford.'"

"True story."

"I went to Northup University, in Bayporte," I told her. "It doesn't have Stanford's reputation or price tag, but up in Canada, it's seen as huge and prestigious, sort of the University of Toronto, West. I remember the pot and beer, the hangovers, the girls and dances and one-nighters and, 'Oh, God, I'm pregnant! What'll we do?'"

"Doesn't sound like much fun," she said.

"It was the best time of my life. Never had so many friends or knew so many girls. I wanted to stay there for the rest of my life."

"Lance has never really shown much interest in anything but golf. He likes girls and his pals and having a good time, of course, but his notion of 'work' and having a purpose in life is hitting a little white ball into a cup and winning trophies and checks. That's not what I had in mind when I raised him."

"How often does Bruce come by to see Lance?"

"Not terribly often. There's emails and phones for that. I'm the one providing most of the in-person moral support. But Bruce will be here for this. We'll have separate rooms, in case you were wondering."

More drinks arrived. I took a long sip of Canadian Comfort over ice and smiled at its burn. Lorna sipped at her white wine. I looked at her, and she at me. You knew you had met someone special when you could comfortably share silence. Lorna and I weren't there yet.

"So," I said, "where are we with that subject that I need to get serious about?"

"That's right—serious. We need to talk about it that way."

"Marni Sandusky says, 'Discrimination is a four-letter word.' I thought it was fourteen."

"See, that's the problem. You're being glib and flippant, making jokes. You're deliberately missing her point. You're making fun of her."

"This place does not discriminate. Women play here all the time," I said.

"But they can't be members," Lorna said.

"So? What have they missed? A bunch of old men swearing and farting."

"There you go again, making fun."

"No, just telling you how it is. We're talking about a private club that can do as it damn well pleases."

"It is *not* a private club," she said, snarling.

"Oh? When did it become public?" I asked.

"This week it's public."

I groaned. "OK, for this week it's a public club. Next week, it will be a private club again. What's wrong with that? Don't you women have private clubs that exclude men? Marni Sandusky is getting her extra-large panties all in a bunch because a certain golf club is a private place and she thinks it should be open to everyone, even though I'm pretty sure she herself doesn't want to join. So the bloggers and TV and radio people jump on the bandwagon and the no-women issue becomes a crime against God. What Marni and the other muckrakers need is another world war or economic collapse so that they can really knock themselves out with a worthwhile cause."

Lorna sat there listening. She didn't get red-faced or tight-mouthed; she simply nodded a bit at what I had to say, as if she'd sat through the same argument before and heard others express it much better.

"Don't get me wrong, Grover. I love the Masters and am delighted to be here. I'm also very proud that my son is competing here. But Marni has a legitimate grievance. There are business honchos whose companies make millions by selling products to women, and yet those women are barred from joining this club that those honchos belong to. I look at that and say to myself, 'That's wrong. It needs to change.'"

"Marni knows that there are other males-only clubs, so how come she's picking on Augusta?"

"Because she thinks it's hypocritical of Augusta to open it up to everyone for one week, then say, 'Sorry, ladies, time's up—go home.'"

"No. She's here to protest because she knows all those TV cameras will be here and they'll give her a chance to bitch and moan for international dissemination."

Lorna gave a little shrug but said nothing.

"There's something else. This whole thing wouldn't be an issue if the club was in New England. It's down here in Dixie, so the liberals like Marni Sandusky are jumping all over it. Marni is ignorant enough to suggest that that they relocate the Masters. Where to? New Haven? Marni Sandusky is a big fat pile of trouble—someone needs to shove a few dozen doughnuts into her mouth and shut the bitch up. Furthermore, I really resent how she's been trashing Augusta's members in the media—making them sound like a bunch of goofy, senile old men who sit around and brag about how much tail they got when they were younger."

"Speech, speech," Lorna muttered.

"Well, what of it? Marni Sandusky is a fat, unhappy woman who gets angry for a living because she can't cope with life. I want to say to her face, 'Yeah, Marni, blame men and golf for all your personal problems.'"

Lorna grinned. "You know what? I think that if you ever get sick of golf, you could always go into public relations. Look, all Marni wants is for Augusta to admit women."

"Oh, and what would that accomplish?"

Lorna shrugged. "A little bit less discrimination and unfairness in the world. That's all. Maybe Marni will fail, Augusta will remain a boys' club and you fellas can go back to your circle jerks or whatever it is you do when the women aren't around."

I sighed. "Augusta should say, 'We've just admitted our first woman. She's a black lesbian in a wheelchair.' That would keep everyone happy for a while."

"All this talk of unfairness, discrimination and hatred is making me hungry," Lorna said. "Let's order dinner."

"And furthermore—"

"Grover?"

"Yes?"

"One more word and you're not getting any nooky tonight."

9

I remembered a bit of some paperback novel that wasn't even worth reading. I had actually bought a few of them over the years, mostly in airports so that I would have something to read during the flight. But I rarely got past the first few chapters. Didn't the authors of such swill know how much they were insulting their readers' intelligence? I usually tossed the novel into the inflight garbage can.

Her full, cherry-red lips. Her hungry tongue. She yearned to devour him whole. (Which part of him? All of him? I think cannibalism is illegal.) *They stroked each other gently, then roughly. They explored each other in ways neither had ever experience.* (Had they never gone to a doctor?) *She kissed his man-nipples, which were turgid with passion.* (I have man-nipples, too. I keep forgetting they're there.) *He thrust his mighty phallus into her, for what seemed eons. They both screamed and cried out, yet remained silent...*

That's when I giggled, or guffawed, or made some other sound.

"Something funny?" Lorna asked me.

"No, nothing. I didn't mean it."

"Something's funny. Tell me."

"Nothing's funny," I said.

"Then tell me why you were laughing."

I shook my head. "It had nothing at all to do with you or what we're doing right now."

"Laughing during sex is inappropriate. It has everything to do with me. Were you laughing *at* me?"

"No, no, no. I was laughing about something I'd read in a novel once."

"So," she said, "you were totally bored with me and let your mind wander off to some novel you'd read. Am I that bad a lay?"

I shook my head some more. "No, it's just that sex is such a sweating, grunting, moaning kind of thing, and they write these novels trying to make it sound elegant and poetic and erotic, and I was sort of listening to us and thinking how *funny* it is when humans get it on. It's like we're just a couple of animals getting it on…"

Her eyes narrowed. "I'm an animal, grunting and groaning for your amusement. I'm so funny that you laughed. How flattering."

"Not at all," I said.

"But you *did* laugh."

"Yes, Lorna, but not at you."

"Oh, was there someone else in this bed you *were* laughing at?"

I groaned.

"Grover," she asked, "do you think I'm one of those pathetic divorced women who needs a mercy fuck from someone like you?"

"Wasn't thinking any such thing." Then, "I was thinking of a trashy novel: 'She kissed the nubs of his man-nipples till they were stiff and hard…'"

She made a face. "'Man-nipples'?"

"Yeah, we got 'em, too. Don't you like man-zoomers? I think they're quite as beautiful as women's. Arnold Schwarzenegger had a great pair when he was young."

"I don't really pay much attention to a man's titties," Lorna said. "He's got other things that interest me more."

"Yeah, that's where men and women are different. Down there, it's all hanging out on a man, whereas with women there's just a patch of hair. But women have these *breasts*, and no two pairs are exactly alike."

"Well," Lorna said, "now I'm in the mood for a cigarette." She reached over, pulled out a Winston from her package and lit it up.

I inhaled her secondhand smoke and almost enjoyed it, even though, as a Canadian, I believed that Americans knew very little about how to make cigarettes and beer. I had quit smoking, after over a decade of twenty cigarettes per day, when I contracted a prolonged case of something from the wheezing hippie who sat next to me on a flight. He wore a soiled T-shirt, tattered jeans, no socks and ancient sandals, and spent most of his time coughing up phlegm into a paper barf bag. Anyway, whatever malady I had acquired from him took me a month to overcome, during which time I felt no desire for a cigarette. By the time I felt well enough to smoke again, I no longer craved cigarettes.

"I didn't mean to offend you," I said to Lorna. "I'm trying to think of the right thing to say at this moment. Please tell me what it is."

"You need to say, 'Gee, Lorna, now you know why I've been divorced three times.'"

10

Picture this: Grover waking up after only a few hours' sleep, after spending the night trying to put things right with the woman who now captivated his soul. There he stands, not unlike a zombie or retard, reminding himself that his shirt goes on top and his pants on bottom. He takes a few bites of the scrambled eggs she has ordered up. He knows he has had far, far too little sleep or food to be at his best, and this is his first morning at the Masters. His tee time is just after eight.

Too bad for him.

But enough of the third-person nonsense. I made it on time because I drove fast, parked my rental car where it didn't belong, and literally ran into the clubhouse to get my golf shoes. I must have looked as badly as I felt as I went to shake hands with Guy.

Luckily, Everett knew what to do about me. If I hadn't called him and didn't show up in the practice area within half an hour of my tee time, check the putting green. If I wasn't there, go to the first tee. If I wasn't *there*, contact the F.B.I.

But I had made it.

"Grover!" Everett said with a wide smile. "Wasn't sure 'bout you this time. Thought I might have to get the Feds involved."

I smiled back. "Not this time, anyway. But you never know with me."

Everett, bless his soul, always put me in the right frame of mind with his gentle good humor. I went to the first tee and hit a perfectly respectable drive that endangered no one. I even made par for that hole. Guy and the Swede had problems. Both ended up in the trees and finished over par.

Later on, as I played consistent, two-under golf, Everett said, "You got everythin' working right, Grover."

"It's that I'm tired," I told him. "You know how a knuckleball pitcher in baseball needs to be exhausted so he won't overthrow? Well, that's me right now. I'm so spent that I'm hitting the ball just right."

"What's our problem today? Hangover?"

"Love hangover," I said.

He smirked. "They're the best kind. Also the worst." Then, "You know this lady well?"

"We just met."

"Is she anyone *I* might know?" he asked.

I grinned. "You'd never believe me."

Everett grinned back. "Try me."

"The Prick's mum."

His jaw dropped. "For real?"

"Would I lie to you?"

"Hope you used a condom."

"I don't take a bath with a raincoat on," I said.

"Don't be a fool, boss."

I kept hitting the ball and it continued to go where I needed it to be. I two-putted on a couple of holes to reach par and ended up with a 68 after 17 holes.

While my name was on the board, so were many others. I hardly expected to be the leader after the first day, especially since Tiger, Phil, Mark and a half-dozen other famous players had done well, too. Surprise, surprise.

I checked my watch—just after two. I felt as if I'd been up for many, many hours; which, of course, I had. I left my iPhone in my car when I golfed, but I did bring my watch. Other golfers wore cheap promotional watches while playing because they were paid to do so; once they got off the course, they chucked those watches and put on their platinum Rolexes or zillion-dollar Patek Philippes.

We had a long wait on the 18th tee. Brian Gay and Russell Henley crept around the trees as officials conferred about rulings.

I stood there, my legs burning and face sweating. I thought for a moment about how little I enjoyed golf when I felt sleepy or hungry. I wanted to, or at least thought I should, start a conversation with the Swede and Norman. After several hours, all I could think of to say was, "Good job it's not raining, hey?"

Both men, well over par, had spent the day driving balls in all the wrong directions, then making clumsy putts that went nowhere near the cup. Throughout, Guy smiled at his poor performance and did little dances whenever his putts finally dropped in. His corpulent missus, Heather, smiled plenty, too. Jumping and waving at her husband, Heather was slapped silly by various parts of her anatomy.

"How did you get here?" I asked. "Whose ass did you kiss?"

"I don't know what you mean," he replied.

"Did you win a tournament somewhere else?"

"Got an invitation in the mail," he told me.

I nodded and we stood silent for a few moments. Then Guy asked the Swede a question.

"You ski the Alps much?"

"I'm Swedish, not Swiss."

"So you don't ski the Alps?"

The Swede glowered at him. "No Alps in Sweden."

"What do you do for exercise in Sweden?" Guy asked.

"Me? I just eat, shit and play golf."

I lost interest in these men's insipid conversation and went to stand next to Everett. Just then, I heard someone's voice.

"You're well under par. Keep doing it!"

"Lorna! Everything OK?"

Now she was dressed in white slacks and a pink crewneck sweater that appropriately hid her zoomers, booty and vag. When I asked her if everything was OK, I meant: Had she slept well and recovered from my ravishing?

She nodded and smiled, looking radiant and beautiful, with no makeup on. I saw a band of freckles across the bridge of her nose that I hadn't noticed.

"Lorna, this is my caddy, Everett Moore. He's also my therapist, spiritual adviser and what else—?"

"Surrogate mother," Everett said.

I nodded. "That's what he does best, and it's what I need most."

They exchanged smiles and nods.

"I'll watch you for a minute," she said. "Then I need to go watch Lance."

"He doing OK with this?" I asked. "He seemed to think it would be too easy."

She shrugged. "He's under par, but he was sneering at the green earlier. I think he's doing fine, but what do *I* know? I'm just his mom."

I smiled. "Yeah, mums are like that."

"Our turn, Grover," said Everett.

"Give me Big Boy," I told him.

"You sure?"

"Give it to me."

He nodded and reached into my bag. He pulled out my best driver. I teed up my ball, got my stance just right, wriggled my bum to show off for Lorna, then swung my hardest. I chuckled with satisfaction at the sound of my clubface smacking the ball. My little Titleist became a tiny spot on the horizon before landing, rolling and settling well onto the fairway. I didn't give it a Lance Priklan monster-whack to within ten feet of the cup, mainly because I lacked his brute strength, but I got all of it. How nice for me.

Lorna let out a delighted little scream and yelled, "Yea, baby!"

I responded with a shrug and grin, as if I'd always teed off that well.

"You took it for a ride that time," Everett said. "Poor ball gonna think you're mad at it."

"My audience inspired me," I said.

After making an easy par, I checked and signed my card in the scorer's tent. Outside, a young woman sports reporter waited for me.

"I'm Kelly Ellard," she said, shaking my hand. "From *Dallas Online*."

She looked to be pushing thirty, and did her best to look like one of the boys: Mavericks jersey, baggy jeans, frizzy brown hair largely untamed.

"They don't want you in the press center for an interview," she said, her voice gentle, as if telling me some heartbreaking news.

"Aw, that's too bad," I retorted. "I guess most of the other reporters are out on the course, following Tiger and Mark and Phil. So you're stuck with me."

She giggled.

"You must be new, Kelly," I said. "I know all the media people at these events, and this is the first time we've met."

"They gave me golf this year. My last gig was the NBA."

"Basketball, eh? Did you like it?"

"Sometimes. I didn't like flying in and out during snowstorms."

"Not many snowstorms happening here in golf," I said.

"It's already fun. Good weather, no night competitions to cover and I don't have to get a crick in my neck interviewing seven-footers."

I gave her what she needed: My bogeys sucked, my pars and birdies rocked, and the wind occasionally became a problem.

"Grover," she said, "I need to ask you this: How do you feel about the women's protest that's coming up?"

"Kelly," I replied, "I don't know *what* their problem is. This is just a gentlemen's game where we hit little white balls into cups. Nobody gets his leg or neck broken or his teeth knocked out, and nobody shoots his ass full of steroids before going out to play."

She laughed. "Well, I can't use any of that, but thanks for sharing. Nice to meet you, Grover."

"We'll talk again."

No one else in the media had any use for me that day. For the rest of that day, I hit practice balls, did some putting or loitered about the contestants' lounge. All the while, I watched as my name slid far down the board. Outdoing myself, I had shot a 68; Tiger Woods and Phil Mickelson were tied at 65; Vijay Singh and some other guy even more obscure than myself had 67s.

"Tiger's got to do better than that," I overheard someone mutter. "Even the nobodies are under seventy."

That summed up a life's effort for me. Pleased to meet you. My name is Grover Bobbitt, but you may call me Mr. Nobody.

11

My score on Friday, an even-par 72, made me eighth overall, and I felt a bit less ridiculous, but Tiger Woods, the leader, seemed his usual cocky, indomitable self. I needed a few very low rounds of my own, and Tiger needed to have a totally incapacitating meltdown in order for me to prevail.

"It's been done before, Grover," said my pal Jake. "Just keep it going. Bear down on Tiger and make him play his best."

I also felt gratified to play like a pro when the two guys I had to play with—Guy Norman and the Swede—still couldn't seem to drive or putt. I mostly stood around and watch them hit into the 90s.

Funny thing was, they both kept laughing and dancing around while I, the pro who actually had a chance at winning this thing, barely cracked a smile even when one of my difficult putts dropped in and the crowd burst out into cheers and applause.

Guy Norman, at the 12th, should have hit his tee ball well over the creek, but it ended up at the edge of the water but remained visible. He could hit it where it lay if he chose to do so.

"I can do this," he said, fondling his wedge. He addressed his ball, with one foot in the water, and slipped into the pond.

The crowd cried out in horror, or delight, or both, as Guy stood waist-deep in the muddy water. Then he stumbled again and became completely submerged.

Some of us rushed to the edge of the pond, more out of curiosity than anything else. Then we heard Heather Norman, his wife, somewhere in the crowd, scream.

"Maybe," Everett said, "she just found out the concession stand is all out of her favorite doughnuts."

I stifled a laugh and peered into the pond. Up he came, struggling out of the water as I tried to decide if he was worth the trouble of saving.

Guy, soaking wet, wrung some of the water out of his clothes and guffawed. "Damn, it's cold in there. Better change my clothes before I catch the flu."

The Swede had problems, too. On the par-five 13th, he hit one of the highest, longest, most spectacular drives I had ever seen at that course; alas, he pulled it so far to the left that it ended up in the trees, flowers and other greenery we all needed to stay out of.

The ball went so far in that I joined the little search party and we tried to find it.

"Here it is!" called the Swede, holding what he claimed was his own ball. He insisted on hitting back into play from there.

I couldn't bear to watch, but did so anyway. I didn't try to talk him out of it, either, and hated myself for it.

The Swede changed mind a dozen times about which club to use. Then he tried out as many stances, and finally got around to the business of trying to hit the ball.

"Waaaah! Naaaaah!"

The Swede, yelping like a dog caught in barbed wire, had swung into a tangled mass of vines, branches and stickers, and could not extricate himself. Everett and a few other caddies went in with their pocketknives and cut him loose.

"I don't need your fucking help!" the Swede cried out, hacking at his ball with one of his irons. "I am a man! I can take care of myself!"

Rivulets of blood, diluted in sweat, ran down his neck and arms. He kept taking the blindest, most vicious cuts at his ball, which moved a few feet here and there.

By and by he got out of trouble. His ball finally dropped into the cup and he bent over to pick it up.

I said, "I think we've all lost count of how many swings you've taken, but they'll probably let you get away with twenty for this hole."

I can still remember the noises he made while thrashing around in the jungle, sounds a grown man with any pride or dignity would never allow himself to make.

"*Arrrrnnngh! Mmmmmmnnnnnoohhh!*"

My pal Gil Donaldo had shot 142, and so had Lance Priklan. Gil smiled about it, while Lance moped around, muttering about what a "dumb-ass course" Augusta turned out to be.

I invited Lance to have a drink with me. I wanted to become better acquainted with him and find out why some people called him "The Prick." Well, I already sort of knew why; I wanted to advise him to think before he said things like, "These Dixie hicks can keep their shitty golf course."

Lance said, "I can sit with you for a quick one, but I need to get back out there and perfect my swing some more."

I nodded, though I didn't understand. I thought golfers merely practiced their swings, then went out there and hit their balls as hard as they could—they didn't "perfect" their swings. I didn't perfect mine, either, because I didn't believe in a "perfect" swing or a "perfect" anything else. But maybe that was why Tiger Woods and Lance Priklan were who they were, while I was the hopelessly "imperfect" Grover Bobbitt.

So we sat and ate sandwiches. I drank beer while Lance slurped down two or three Diet Cokes. He swallowed a big mouthful of food and asked, "What's up with you and my mom?"

I made a face. "Excuse me?"

"I'm glad you're boffing her. She needs it."

I knew that in California the "boffing" of women who "needed it" happened countless times every night (and often during the day), just as it happened sometimes in my native Canada, too. However, I wasn't altogether aware that those California women's sons made it their business to ask the boffers about the boffing.

"Lance," I said, careful not to answer his question, "why would you ask me such a thing?"

He shrugged. "You're a pro golfer. You're different. Ever since my mom called it quits with my dad, she's pretty much kept to herself. But when she does go out, it's been with money men and other clowns who bore her."

"Your mum is a beautiful woman," I told him. "I've enjoyed getting to know her. You *know* what a lovely lady she is, don't you?"

"I don't look at her that way. She's my mom. She's old."

"Has she been serious about anyone? Those money men and other clowns?"

"Nope. She goes out with them a few times and that's it. She says they're all the same. They just want to hear, 'Wow! You're fascinating! Tell me more about yourself!' She doesn't have much use for those kinds of people."

"She needs to stay away from the high-tech entrepreneurs and other Silicon Valley guys," I said. "Say, Lance, when your parents were together, did you have any sense that they were unhappy?"

"When they were together," he said, "she did her thing, he did his and I did mine. Mine was always golf."

"So you were pretty much unaware of how they felt about each other until they separated."

"Oh, there were raised voices sometimes or days of silence. I think the fact that my dad craved sex with a variety of women had something to do with their marital problems."

"I suppose he just never got laid enough in high school," I said.

"Too bad for him," Lance said.

My pal Jake Grimsley missed the cut by exactly one shot, which is one of the most painful experiences a professional golfer can have. *One shot!* He thinks back to all those rounds he's just played, those putts that just refused to go in or drives that simply refused to go far enough, and he wants to whack himself with his eight-iron.

One fucking shot!

Jake packed his suitcases and got ready to go back home to Medford, Oregon. His wife, Bev, hadn't come with him. She had never been to a golf tournament, or much of anywhere else. Bev didn't travel, not even to the local shopping mall, out of fear of being raped. (I had seen a picture of her; nobody but Jake would even give her a second look.) The last time I'd seen her, a dozen years earlier at a tournament in New Jersey, she insisted that her husband drive her to the emergency room at the nearest hospital because she believed she was having a heart attack or stroke, or both. When I asked about her later, Jake told me the doctors said she'd had an anxiety attack. Jake wanted to get back home to pet his two big poodles, whom he dearly missed.

Jake, a classy guy, made a memorable departure from town. Gil Donaldo and I walked him back to his vehicle. First he kicked his Ford Explorer so hard that he put a big dent in the driver's-side door. Then he opened the SUV's rear doors and threw his clubs inside with red-faced rage. Finally, he walked over to the nearest magnolia patch, hauled out his dingus and took a nice long piss on the beautiful flowers.

"That's very intelligent, Jake," I told him, amazed at his remarkable timing in pulling such a stunt when no one happened to be looking. Urinating on the magnolias? That could get you punched out by another member.

"I missed the cut by one shot, motherfucker," he muttered to nobody in particular as he got in and drove off.

12

I sat with my pal Gil Donaldo in a pancake house close to the golf course. I have never been a vegetarian nor one who believes in eating things I don't like even though those things are supposed to benefit my vital organs or keep my hemorrhoids small. At the pancake house I ate scrambled eggs, sausage, pancakes and potatoes. I also drank four cups of coffee.

The women protestors would be demonstrating directly across the street, according to the sheriff's office. Gil and I had arrived at that pancake house early because Lorna told me that some news crews, in town to cover the women's protest, were using that restaurant as their hangout while waiting for Marni Sandusky and her followers spouted off about what pigs men were.

Gil and I wanted to check it out because we were too young to go to Kent State or Berkeley and see real rabble-rousing and shit-disturbing for ourselves.

"I need to see this," I'd said to Lorna, "because I've had many women scream at me about golf in private, I've never witnessed hundreds of women scream about golf in public."

"You're a funny guy," she retorted, "but looks aren't everything."

Sitting there in the pancake house, I said to Gil, "The fans must be happy when they look at the leader board. Tiger's on top. Steve Stricker and Phil Mickelson are up there, too."

Tiger was at seven under par. A few others were at six under, including Thom Knutson, my old acquaintance who had once been a friend. Thom was a brainless wonder during his first Tour. I taught him a few things—like the fundamentals of golf—and urged him not to swear so much while on the course. He ignored my advice about getting his hair cut—he was very vain about his tameless mop of blond hair —and he refused to wear loose pants that hid his many prodigious erections.

Through me, he met my cute friend Vanessa, a Canadian Airways flight attendant. He married her and fathered her two children. He respected and admired his wife so much that he boffed his way into divorce court. It cost him much of his fortune, and she rebounded by marrying my close friend Strom Budman, a dozen-year veteran of the Tour. He had been ogling her goodies for some time. Once her divorce became final, she became both single *and* rich. So Strom left the Tour for a while so he could chase her.

Thom Knutson ended our friendship after winning his second major. He started eating retard sandwiches and decided that I was no longer worthy of his time and attention.

Thom's best friend swung between his legs. He called his penis Ernest. I had met other men who named theirs, too. Usually they chose Peter, Dick or Rod. Johnson and Woody, too. But Ernest?

I knew ladies who had met Ernest. Thom showed me notes women had written to Ernest. "How you hanging, Ernest? Or are you?" and "Ernest, tell Thom he's the best-equipped golfer in the business."

Gil Donaldo said we should write an illustrated children's book about Ernest and call it *The Human Anaconda*. Easy money.

Since I had been difficult to locate over the past few nights, Gil started in on me about Lorna.

"What's the deal with her, man? Where did she grow up? What does she do when she's not watching The Prick play golf? What kind of person is she, really?"

"She is a fine American and a really lovely human being," I told him.

"What do *you* know about great Americans? You're a Canadian," he said.

"She's a lovely person," I repeated.

"I don't think it's her personality you're so interested in. Are you with her most evenings?"

"Yes. We watch TV and order in from room service."

"I wonder what The Prick thinks of all this," he said.

"He is delighted that his mum is keeping company with a gentleman friend."

He smirked. "You're a funny guy—"

"But looks aren't everything."

We both laughed as we kept on eating breakfast.

13

At the site of the protest, we saw men on stilts whose signs said WE'RE ABOVE IT ALL, meaning Marni Sandusky's nonsense. Some Elvis impersonators stood around in garish jumpsuits and shiny wigs; for a moment, I thought I was in Memphis.

I went up to an Elvis and asked, "What's he got to do with golf?"

"Just everything." The man twisted his lip and spoke in an Elvis twang, which sounded not at all like The King.

"Elvis liked golf? I've never heard that one," I said.

"He *loved* it, man." The impersonator sounded a bit more confident.

"But I never saw him play, and I knew his life fairly well."

"Don't gotta *play* it to *love* it, fella. He wasn't much on the gittar but he loved *it*, too."

"I think I understand," I said.

"All righty, then."

Gil Donaldo stepped in. "Elvis Presley had no interest in golf. He didn't know which end of a golf club went where, and he didn't care. He would have said, 'Hey! This would make a great sex toy!' Later on in life, he was too fat and strung out on pills to take up any hobby aside from eating and sleeping. As for singing or playing the 'gittar,' he couldn't do either worth shit, but that didn't hold him back professionally."

The three Elvises looked at each other, shrugged and started humming different songs at the same time.

We listened for a few moments, got bored and went over to the TV crews, demonstrators and police.

I went straight over to the emaciated hippie with the scraggly beard and unwashed, shoulder-length hair. His ancient T-shirt bore some faded message; his jeans looked my age. His handmade sign read GOD HATES GOLF. He stood against a tree.

Gil went up to him and said, "Groovy sign, man."

The hippie smiled. "Glad you like it."

"Where you at right now?" Gil asked. "Just being?"

The hippie shook his head. "No, man, I'm just tryin' to get my head straight so I can do a lecture and tell the people what's goin' on when the demonstration starts."

"What you gonna tell 'em?" Gil wanted to know.

"Just that golf destroys our humanity and corrupts our morals. We set aside all that precious land so that rich people can hit little balls into holes, and it's just not right. We need for everyone to wake up and see how bad golf is. Otherwise, our whole country may become one big golf course."

"I hear ya, brother," Gil said, nodding. "You need to get that message out. Golf *will* fuck us all up if we let it."

My iPad said that Marni Sandusky would arrive at noon to speak to her crowd as a sort of warmup exercise. We waited for her by hanging out in the outdoor-seating area of the donut shop. At one table sat a few pallid, buffed-up skinheads with swastikas carved between their eyes; at another sat the sheriff's deputy.

For a while we eavesdropped on Deputy Sheriff D.B. Costello, whose paunch indicated that he and this donut shop were real good buddies. Between bites of a honey cruller, he spoke to some people who resented the presence of the skinheads at the next table. The skinheads had brought a sign saying WHITE IS RIGHT.

"No," the deputy said, "I can't shoo them skinheads any more than I can do anythin' about those fellas on stilts or that smelly hippie over there. This is America, a free country. Everybody gonna have their say and then everybody gonna go home or play golf or whatever. But we all gonna be nice boys and girls while the protest is happenin'."

"How many protestors will be here today?" someone asked.

"Well, we got some here already, maybe a dozen or twenty. Yesterday they were talkin' about a few thousand, so I'm thinkin' it might be closer to one hundred."

"I don't see any protesters here now," said someone else."

The deputy sheriff pointed to a big platform. "See over there? All them girlies that look like fellas? One of them is Marni Sandusky's press secretary. The one that looks like a linebacker."

We looked in that direction for several moments.

One of the reporters said, "I guess we won't be seeing many *Sports Illustrated* swimsuit models here today."

"I guess you're right," retorted the deputy sheriff.

"Marni's here!" someone hollered as a big white Lincoln Town Car stopped at the vacant field.

Just then, Lorna showed up, emerging from the crowd.

"Grover!" she called out. "Aren't you supposed to be hitting golf balls?"

"That can wait. My tee time is this afternoon. We wanted to see Marni Sandusky and hear her speak."

Lorna shook her head. "Nothing's happening today. It's all postponed till tomorrow, when the golf crowd will be bigger."

I frowned. "Who told you that?"

"Marni's press secretary."

"The linebacker?"

"Excuse me?"

"The deputy sheriff called Marni's press secretary a linebacker."

"I ought to send the press secretary over there to kick that cop's ass," Lorna said.

A woman who looked androgynous enough to be Marni Sandusky bounded up the platform steps and nodded at all the cheering women. She stood at the microphone, surrounded by a few other strapping non-males who presumably were bodyguards, as if Marni needed protection.

"Let's go check her out," I said.

Marni Sandusky was a big human being, tall and broad across. She wore yards of denim and pounds of jade jewelry. Her designer eyeglasses seemed too small for her large, round face, and her graying bangs looked greasy and dull.

She reiterated her usual sentiments, namely what an outrage Augusta committed upon America each day. Didn't the country know that all those Masters people were CEOs of companies that sold products to women, and yet women were barred from membership in the club…?

A reporter yelled, "What advice do you have for the golfers' wives here?"

"My advice," replied Marni, "is for them to say to their husbands, 'If we don't get any women into the club, *you* aren't getting any from now on!'"

Deafening cheers and applause greeted Marni's response.

"Who," Marni Sandusky now wanted to know, "will be by my side tomorrow when I walk up to that awful place and demand some justice for women everywhere? Who will do that with me?"

"Me, me, me!" the women all yelled.

I turned to Lorna and said, "It's not so awful at the golf course. It smells nice and everyone is well dressed."

She made a face. "Having fun?"

I cackled.

A guy very near the stage shouted, "Marni! Fix me something to eat!" I knew right away he was Liam Hubbell, and next to him stood Gil Donaldo.

"Fix my fence!" she replied.

"Do my laundry!"

"Mow my lawn!" Marni said.

"Wash my windows!"

"Repair my roof!" Marni shot back.

"Give me head!"

"I've heard enough," yelled Deputy Sheriff D.B. Costello as he rushed forward and grabbed Liam and Gil by their necks. "I won't be havin' *that* kind of talk on *my* watch. No sign here sayin' POTTY MOUTHS WELCOME."

Hubbell said, "But Deputy, we were just trying to bring some levity to the protest."

As the deputy dragged the men through the crowd, Hubbell saw me and said, "Hey, Grover!"

Gil also said, "What's happening, Grover?"

I nodded hello, and they disappeared.

Lorna said, "Friends of yours, Grover?"

14

Clark Irving of the Boston *Globe* said, "Grover, you would make a good Sunday column for me. You should feel flattered. I'm online, and everyone who matters reads me."

His assessment of his popularity wasn't that huge an exaggeration. At that point in American journalism's history, Clark Irving had achieved major prominence as a *Globe* columnist and bestselling author. Who cared that Clark had become one of his country's most annoying writers in his column, and in his books he came notorious for his ability to be both pompous and inaccurate. To Clark, the truth was whatever he wanted it to be.

"Grover," he said, "let's go up to the clubhouse, talk about your sixty-nine over a drink, and discuss your feelings about the fact that you still don't have a chance in hell of winning this thing."

Clark smiled as he said that last part, as if to assure me that he'd meant it as a *joke*, son.

Before sitting down with him, I had done some very brief interviews with local and cable TV personalities, all of whom were deeply infatuated with their own voices. They asked me their questions, answered them for me, then said, "Grover, would you agree with that?" So I would say, "Yeah, Leah. Nice talking to you." End of interview.

Clark and I sat at a table on the veranda. I ordered a pitcher of iced tea for us. He reached into his leather bag and pulled out a copy of his latest bestseller.

"Long time, no see, Grover. I brought you this book because I'm not sure if you've read it yet. This one's signed."

The book was *Juicing: How Today's 'Poison' Will Become Tomorrow's Vitamin.*

"You're much too kind," I said, perusing the title of the book I knew I would never read. "I've looked everywhere for it but they were always sold out."

"So," Clark said, "let's talk about the Masters."

"Let's not and say we did," I retorted.

He laughed. "I can use that."

"Be my guest."

"Do you think you can win this time?" he asked, scribbling on his yellow legal pad.

"Well, I'm on the board, so that's a good sign."

He nodded. "You did well with that sixty-seven. You were under par on some pretty difficult holes. On the twelfth you made a long putt that I was sure you'd miss. Anyway, that's all the time I have for the play-by-play. I need to file my story by eight o'clock."

"Want to know why I can't win these majors? It's very simple: Tiger, Phil, Mark, etcetera."

Clark smirked. "Blaming those big guns for your own failures? Yummy." He scribbled some more.

"Those 'big guns' have me by a few strokes. I'm playing my best—unfortunately, so are they."

Clark shook his head. "You're full of juicy quotes today, Grover."

"Hey, guy, I seem to be doing your job. So why don't you grab some clubs and play for me tomorrow?"

He ignored my remark. "How old are you, Grover? Forty-two, forty-three?"

I snarled a bit. "Just turned forty."

Clark frowned, as if doing some mental arithmetic. "You've been out here for damn near two decades, right? Always a bridesmaid, never a bride." He smiled. "You've won a dozen minors but never a major."

"Is that a question?"

"You won the Players not long ago. Right?"

"Right."

"But the Players is a minor. You have never won a major. Will you ever win a major?"

"Gee, Clark, I sure hope not. I mean, I'm just having *so* much fun coming all the way down here so that I can finish fifth in the Masters, like I did once. I've also finished third in the PGA and in the top ten twice in the British Open. If the guys like Tiger and Phil would retire, I could win a major or two."

Clark paused. He had scribbled it all down. "Who do you play cards with here?"

I shrugged. "Nobody here plays cards."

"Why not?"

"Because they have better things to do."

"Like what?" he asked.

"Oh, like seeing their therapists, agents and tax attorneys. Or maybe sending their wives out shopping so they can boff the babysitters." I added, "I don't suppose you can use any of that."

"I suppose you're right. Well, who are your best friends?"

"Mostly people from back home in Canada. People from Oliver Johnson High School and Northup University, like Red Crossley and Flash Gortton. In the golf world, Gil Donaldo, Jake Grimsley…Strom Budman, too."

"Where's Strom these days? What's he up to?"

"He's happier than a pig in shit. He's in Florida with Vanessa and her money. Their estate is bigger than many airports."

"I didn't know she had gotten that much money from her divorce. I didn't know Knutson had that much money to cough up."

"Well, he had it. Now it's hers."

"And Strom's," Clark added.

I nodded. "As long as he minds his manners, keeps her happy and they stay married, it's his to enjoy too."

"Now, you and Thom Knutson were chummy for quite a while. Many say that you taught him much of what he knows about golf. I know you and he had some personal issues. Are you guys still friends, or what?"

"We're polite in front of the media. He's really come into his own."

"Meaning…?"

"Well," I said, "he used to be a wannabe douche bag, and now he's major-league douche bag."

"He's got a beautiful new girlfriend. They're practically engaged. Have you two been introduced?"

I nodded. "She's a Russian rapper. Her stage name is Soviette. I can't remember her real name. It has something like twelve syllables."

I had trouble getting my mind around a Russian rapper, especially a blonde woman, but maybe it made some sense. Rap music, or hip hop, or whatever you wanted to call it, came from the blacks in America's ghettos. They created and used it as their way of expressing their agony and anger over being oppressed.

"Grover," Clark was asking now, "would you mind if I asked you why you and Helene divorced? I ask as an empathic friend, not a nosy journalist."

"Helene," I told him, "was an exploitative, manipulative, opportunistic cunt who was out for Number One at all times. And those were her *good* qualities."

Clark burst out laughing. "Grover," he said, "you really bust my onions sometimes."

"Well," I continued, "if I haven't won a major yet, I've still made more than my share of money. We had plenty of assets, and I just said, 'Fuck it—take whatever you want. I just want to get out of this marriage.' So she gathered up our assets and buggered off."

"I'm going to use all of that, OK?"

"Go ahead. Just make sure you spell my name right."

15

When I played golf at Northup University many years ago, my friends on the football team told me that their coaches urged them to be celibate before each game. The coaches believed that women weakened the players' bodies or made them less aggressive. Others said that sex before a competition often made the competitor perform better, because the competitor now had someone to show off for.

For myself, I liked my loving whenever I could get it, even—especially?—before a competition.

After I called room service and told them what we wanted brought up for dinner, Lorna said to me, "You're showing off right now in a couple of ways."

"That's good, isn't it?"

"And I'm showing off for you," she said.

"You don't need to show off for me. I'm already quite taken with you," I told her.

"We're showing off for each other, Grover. What does that mean to you?"

"Search me, man."

"Where do you think our relationship is headed? What will become of us?"

I shrugged. "We will live until we die. Beyond that, I haven't a clue."

"You're quite a deep thinker," she said.

"I have my moments. Say, has Lance asked you about why you're never in your own room at night?"

She shook her head. "He doesn't ask those kinds of questions."

I smiled. *Have you been boffing my mom, Grover? I'm OK with it if you are. She needs it.* "Doesn't he ask you about that Canadian weirdo you seem to be spending lots of time with?"

"He *does* ask me what I'm doing each night. I tell him I'm having dinner with friends. He says, 'Nice for you. Have fun, Mom.' He has dinner with other golfers. Then he comes back to the hotel early. He watches some TV, calls a few of his girlfriends on his iPhone, and goes to bed."

"Since he's young, tall, handsome, successful and rich, I assume the chicks are all over his butt like tight jeans."

She nodded. "But the thing is, in some ways he's really not that great a catch. He's a golf freak. It's really the only thing he wants to talk about. If this or that girlfriend goes out with him and she doesn't know about Tiger Woods and Phil Mickelson and the Masters, she'll just yawn and daydream, that's the end of *her.*"

Just then, the room-service waiter knocked on the door. Lorna, in her birthday suit, slipped into the washroom. I signed for our meals and left far too big a tip.

"I thought he'd never leave," Lorna said as she came back out and put on her underwear. We ate dinner—she had a chicken Caesar salad and I wolfed down a Denver omelet—and talked about the leaderboard.

The top 10 looked like this after 54 holes:

```
Tiger Woods............65-72-70-207
Phil Mickelson.................66-72-69-207
Ferret Chalmers..........66-73-68-207
Ken Duke.................. 67-71-70-208
```

```
Harris English............70-69-69-208
Thom Knutson...........69-69-70-208
Gary Woodland..........71-66-72-209
Grover Bobbitt...........68-72-69-209
Sumner Froggert.........67-74-68-209
Mason Duthie............70-69-72-211
```

Not far below those guys were Gil Donaldo and Lance Priklan at 213.

"Lance is six strokes back," Lorna noted. "He would have to shoot something incredible tomorrow to stay in this thing."

I shook my head. "It's not about Lance or the six strokes. It's about those fourteen guys ahead of him. They would all need to have a really shitty day while Lance was having a really great day. That's pretty rare."

"Tell me about this Gil Donaldo guy. Lance is paired with him tomorrow."

"Who are you more interested in tomorrow, Marni Sandusky or the golfers?"

"I *will* be at the rally. I promised Marni I'd hear the speeches. I'll also be following two golfers. Now, what about Gil Donaldo?"

"Oh, he's just a good-natured boy from the Midwest. Sioux City, Iowa, I believe. He decided early on that he would rather play golf than work for a living."

"My father was born in Sioux City," Lorna said.

"No kidding?"

"It's the truth. His daddy was a railroad engineer who died young, so his mom and the rest of them moved to California, because that's what Okies did when they had a huge setback."

"Sort of like *The Grapes of Wrath*," I said.

"Except we were luckier and better off than the Joad family," Lorna said. "Anyway, he ended up in Los Angeles, where he met my mother, who wanted to be a movie star but spent her life as an office flunky at Paramount."

"I'll bet she met her share of other young lovelies who aspired to become movie stars," I said.

Lorna sighed. "Many applied, but only a few got film careers."

"I'm Canadian, and I used to be proud of the fact that one of the greatest stars ever, Mary Pickford, was also a Canadian. But then, she moved down here and never went back to Canada. The American have this 'brain drain' thing where they take Canada's best people."

"Let's get back to Gil Donaldo."

"Right. Gil is younger than I am, and I don't really know what we have in common besides golf. He went to the University of Iowa, where he played golf and football. We've played several tournaments together and he's always been a friend to me. His wife is Charmaine. They met while they were students at the U., and live out in some exclusive Dallas suburb."

"Gil sounds like a decent enough man."

"He spends most of his time flying out to golf tournaments. They have a teenager who plays every sport you can imagine, and Charmaine drives him to his practices. Gil says that she was the shame of her sorority because she tipped the scales at one-twenty-six and everyone called her 'Fatso.'"

"She'll hate them for the rest of her life."

"Not at all. She thought it was funny."

"They sound like a couple with a sense of humor."

"Yeah," I said. "That's why I like him. He's crude but funny as hell."

"Do you like crude people? Crude humor?"

I shrugged. "Yeah, I suppose. I mean, I don't like upright, uptight, politically correct people." I paused. "I mean, when we first met, you were there at the Masters with your titties sticking out and your bush almost visible in those tight jeans. You're a beautiful woman with a wonderful body, but you're no kid. You have crow's feet and lines around your mouth, and you were dressed like some slutty chick, and you were being *so* politically incorrect. I fucking loved it! Then I found out that the slutty chick was Priklan's mum, and I loved it even more. But you already knew that. We've already had this conversation."

"Yes, we have. But it was nice hearing all of that again."

16

Later that evening, after Lorna and I had pleasured each other, I received the break-a-leg call from Strom Budman and Vanessa.

"We're not in Florida," Strom said. "We have a place on Coronado Island."

"Lucky you," I said.

"When we get sick of this," he went on, "we may head up north to Mercer Island, near Seattle."

"Take me with you."

"After that, we were thinking of flying out to Spain."

"You can keep Spain," I said. "I've nearly died there a couple of times from eating native Spanish cuisine."

He wished me luck and said he sincerely hoped I would be able to break my jinx and win that major I so craved.

"Anyway, Grover," he said, "I want to share my own good news with you. Do you remember Kevin and Warren, Vanessa's two boys?"

I did, unfortunately; she'd had them with Thom Knutson, and everyone called their little brats "the two stooges." Strom had the good sense to enroll the two sociopaths in a Maryland military academy that, over five years, ended the boys' backtalk and insolence and molded them into moderately acceptable young men.

"I've gotten the boys accepted into Bellis College in Connecticut! Grover! Isn't that terrific?"

He added, quite without shame, that he'd made a seven-figure donation to Bellis College to make sure that his stepsons would enter that prestigious school in September. Bellis, a "highly progressive" college, according to its catalog, offered students the opportunity to design their own curriculum and even grade themselves. English, math, history? That was yesterday's stuff.

Kevin would spent his four years—and many thousands of dollars of his mother's money—reading whatever he fancied and writing papers out it. Warren would surely do something similar.

"Congratulations," I said. "Your boys deserve it."

"Grover! This is Vanessa!" said a familiar voice. "Is she someone I'd like to meet?"

"Excuse me?"

"Whoever is there with you right now," she said. "Would I like her?"

"There's nobody here, Vanessa. Why do you assume there is?"

She laughed. "Because if you were alone, you wouldn't be sitting there in your room. You'd be out there hitting golf balls."

"Congratulations," I said, "on shaking down that goof Knutson, marrying a good man and owning half the world."

She laughed. "Thanks. Now answer my question. The lady with you right now? Is she a possible Missus Bobbitt number four?"

"You never know, Vanessa. You just never know."

"Well, I hope she is, and that she's Miz Right. You deserve it. And Grover?"

"Mmm?"

"Helene was *such* a cunt. I'm sorry it took you that long to figure it out. I know it also cost you a bunch of money."

"Oh, well. Too bad for me."

17

All the fucked-up bullshit started when I was trying to tee up on the ninth hole.

I will remember it forever, just as I'll remember where I was and what I was doing when 9/11 happened, or when Elvis or John Lennon died, or when my parents died. The day the 49ers won their first Super Bowl. The things that really matter in life.

In retrospect, one would think that the people who ran the Masters and the police department would have anticipated possible trouble and been ready to deal with it. But I guess that nobody suspected that Marni Sandusky had friends and supporters who wanted to help her infiltrate the Masters.

Marni Sandusky's fiat astonished me. An admission ticket to the Masters is always an extraordinarily difficult item to obtain, and yet I saw at least a hundred protestors wearing legal Masters credentials. I couldn't imagine who'd supplied them with those creds. What I *did* know was that they were there, in my way, and a simple "Please step aside, ma'am, so I don't whack you with my driver" wouldn't do.

I felt deeply relieved that Lorna Priklan was absent from this chaos. She had to hear the speeches, and once she concluded that she'd already heard everything worthwhile, she left.

So did everyone else, and Marni Sandusky wanted it that way.

My day had started off poorly, too. I had to eat breakfast with my agent, Barney Smoltz. He had flown in from Los Angeles, where he had immersed in the troubles of another important client, Coleman Trey of the Lakers.

For months, Coleman had been in and out of court because of a pair of rape charges. He had retained the services of a pretty and prestigious attorney, Steffany Rachelson, who made frequent TV appearances to explain legal proceedings in layman's terms. But Steffany knew that Coleman's case was a toughie. Coleman, invited to a Los Angeles high school to demonstrate how a typical rape might occur, got turned on and carried away. As the roomful of female students sat and watched, Coleman threw the teacher, a pleasant-looking thirtyish woman, over a chair and banged her silly. Then he went to town on a sixteen-year-old student, pinning her to a desk. After two dozen delays, the case went to trial, and the jury took only minutes to acquit the world-famous jock.

Barney Smoltz shook his head and laughed. "Poor Coleman, he's so pissed off over going to court and being treated like a common criminal. He thought superstars like him never got arrested. He said, 'This legal system better not be fuckin' with me again or I'll change my name to Yomama bin Lotta and start bombin' buildings and shit.'"

Barney brought me tax documents that almost made me cry.

"How can it be," I asked him, "that I owe so much money?"

"It's because," he replied, "you earned most of your income in this country, which has the biggest, meanest, most buffed-out war machine in the history of the world."

I nodded. "OK, I accept the fact that America needs

her war machine to protect Canada. But I resent paying taxes so that some guy on welfare can buy a Cadillac."

They had paired me with Stu Claudell, which meant that if I ever learned of a village that needed an idiot, I knew just the guy to recommend.

Stu Claudell, a proud Auburn University alumnus, had a daddy who was the boss of that city's largest law firm. At his wedding, Stu wore a blue tuxedo with an orange bow tie (Auburn's school colors); his heiress bride, Cookie, wore a blue gown with orange trim. Her bridesmaids wore blue dresses and orange shoes; his groomsmen wore Auburn jerseys and orange wristbands. When the preacher asked, "Who gives this woman to this man?" the bride's industrialist daddy replied, "Her daddy, mama and the Auburn University Tigers. May they win many more national titles and make us all very, very proud."

Stories about Stu and Cookie's blue-and-orange wedding made golfers laugh in locker rooms all over America, and probably Canada, too. Some men said that Cookie Claudell, Southern belle and rich lady, liked to ride unfamiliar dicks when her hubby was away.

Stu and I heard Marni's racket as we got ready to tee off at the ninth hole, which was located near the clubhouse.

I pictured Marni Sandusky and her many supporters standing at the golf course's main entrance, waving their signs and shouting above each other, hoping to be heard by the chairman and some of the complacent old men in green jackets and cops who stood there to make sure the big, angry women didn't frighten the old men.

I saw from the TV news footage later on that I had it right. The protestors chanted, "Hey hey, ho ho, discrimination has got to go!" and waved signs saying TIME TO EMANCIPATE WOMEN and WAKE UP, AMERICA!

"What bullshit," Stu said to me on the fairway. "Those old hags have nothing better to do than make trouble for us. Don't they know that this our workplace and that we need to feed our families just like other men?"

I nearly laughed. Stu's daddy was rich, and his daddy-in-law even richer. He scarcely needed the money he was playing for. He golfed for a living because he didn't want to work. The sports reporters loved it when, during interviews, we indicated that we honestly thought that golf was job, not a game. I wanted to say, "Stu, if you think golf is hard, try sitting at a computer eight hours a day or man the lunch counter. Better yet, try fixing people's cars all day till you stink of oil and grease. *That's* work."

The thing *I* regretted about the protestors and their commotion was that they interrupted my flow. I had been playing, thinking and feeling well that day, and I'd be the first to admit that I often defeated myself with a shit attitude.

At that point, I shared the lead with Tiger and Phil. When that happened, all I could think was, *Don't think about it. Just play golf.*

Stu and I stood at the ninth, sneering at the cup whose mouth seemed to be laughing at us. And why shouldn't the little bastard mock us? The green was uneven; a poorly putted ball could roll back to the poor doofus who'd tapped it.

Tiger, what would *you* do?

Thom Knutson and Harris English stood waiting back at the ninth tee. At the eighth green were Justin Rose and Ken Duke. Down the eighth fairway were High and Mighty themselves, Tiger and Phil.

Several groups ahead of me, on the eleventh, were Gil Donaldo and Lance Priklan. Therefore, Lorna Priklan, golf lover and golf mother, was hustling between the two sections of the golf course, cheering on her son and the man with whom she'd lately been having room-service dinners and hot, sweaty desserts.

Lance's name had been missing from the leaderboard throughout the day, so I knew he was swinging and putting with rookie anxiety; plus, he had simply underestimated the challenges of Augusta. I could imagine him practically throwing a temper tantrum over the speedy greens and the humid Southern air, while Gil, gnashing his teeth in frustration, fought the temptation to give Lance a golf-club enema.

On the ninth tee, I looked around and saw Lorna. I smiled and she smiled back. I flexed my right arm in imitation of Lance, which she knew meant, *How's the big boy doing?*

She rolled her eyes and grabbed her throat. I nodded and shrugged. The big boy was choking at the Masters. His drives were crooked and his putts weren't dropping in.

Been there, done that.

Stu, the only man out there who considered golf honest work, hit his ball to the ninth green as I stood and watched. His facial muscles twitched and he struck his ball much too hard. It flew past the cup and stopped at the end of the green. Stu, well over par already, blew out a huge sigh and wiped some sweat off his forehead.

"Yeah, fucker! Go roll on home to Auburn! See if I give a good goddamn!" He yelled loudly enough for me, Everett and many protestors to hear him.

The really awful and dreadful thing about *my* shot to the green was that I had hit my ball just right. I heard the juicy little *thwack* and beamed as my Titleist bounced and rolled on its merry way to the cup.

"Go, baby!" cried Everett. "Do it for Daddy!"

"Don't touch!" I yelled.

My ball would have dropped in or stopped within a couple of feet, for an easy putt. But we'll never know, because at the moment my ball stopped bouncing and began rolling, dozens of protestors charged onto the fairway.

They swarmed about, making ungodly noises while they did some weird kind of bird dance. I wondered if one or two would drop her drawers, squat and make doo-doo on the lovely green grass.

I shook my head at all their freakiness, then heard similar noises in the distance and realized that these women were disrupting Tiger and Phil, too, and probably Lance.

Later on, I learned that some of the women in this or that group had picked up players' balls on the fairway or green and lobbed them into the trees. They needn't have bothered; under the rules, the players had the right, with impunity, to place their new balls where their old ones had been.

Still, the ladies wriggled and chirped. Golfers should enjoy themselves that much.

Everett and I walked up to the green as the siren blared, the way it did when lightning became a threat, and the demonstrators took off. They just beat it, disappearing into the wall of trees and out the other side to the parking lot. Some of them, too fat or slow, were taken down by security guards or golf fans.

Everett and I held our sides as we laughed at the sight of flabby protestors' being tackled, football style, then slapped and punched by sweating, wheezing guards.

"I bet those guards thought they wouldn't have to do anything like that today," I said to Everett.

"Yeah, but they're lovin' every minute of it," he said.

But I stopped laughing when I got to where my ball was supposed to be. It was gone.

18

After the silliness had ended and the protestors removed from the golf course—the police said that those crazy women had committed an infraction but the Masters bosses refused to press charges—Grand Wizard Marni Sandusky of Women Who Hate Golf and the Men Who Loved It told the media that her bit of civil disobedience was good but not enough. "There will be more," she promised or threatened, and left town.

James Morrison Weatherby DuPree, the rules official assigned to our group, was the vice-president of some golf association. I wondered how much of a chance I stood with a guy who had a name that long.

DuPree's first interviewee, Ellis Royman, was a craggy faced old fart wearing old shorts and older sneakers. Royman's snapback cap said PENNZOIL.

"Where did you find Mister Bobbitt's ball?" DuPree asked.

"Like I told you before," said Royman. "I found 'er in the bunker just off the green. She was half-buried in the ground, like someone had stomped on 'er."

"Sir, did you see Mister Bobbitt's ball enter the bunker?" DuPree scratched his chin. He'd told everyone, many times, that his people had come over on the Mayflower, as if that somehow made him better than the rest of us.

Royman shook his head. "No, I did not."

"Then why did you decide to go looking for Mister Bobbitt's ball in the bunker?"

"Because," Royman said, "that's where most balls end up, so that's where you start looking. Most of my balls are in the bunkers or the rough more often than they're on the fairway or the green."

"Mister Royman," asked DuPree, "where were you standing when you watched Mister Bobbitt hit his golf ball into the bunker?"

"Hold it!" I exclaimed. "Mister Royman did not see me hit my ball into the bunker because I did not hit it there. As a matter of fact, I made a wonderful shot that might have gone in until a protestor grabbed it and threw it away. I believe that's called an 'outside influence,' and therefore I'm entitled to place the ball within a reasonable distance of the cup."

"But," said DuPree, "we don't know for sure about this 'outside agency.'"

"*I* know it," I told him. "I know it for an absolute fact."

"No, you don't," said DuPree. "Neither do I. That's what we're here to determine."

I resisted the temptation to ask, "Are you from one of those country clubs a person can't join if they've ever *worked* for a living?"

What I said was, "My ball was heading straight for the cup. Ask anyone who was there. Ask Stu Claudell. Stu, tell 'em how it was."

Stu shrugged. "I didn't watch you hit it. I had my mind on other things."

"Way to go, Stu," I said.

Everett came to the rescue. "Mistuh DuPree, he's tellin' the truth. We had a great lie and no wind and he made a real fine shot. You *know* Grover Bobbitt hasn't hit one into the bunker in a mighty long time."

"I do *not* know that Mister Bobbitt has stayed out of

the bunkers. To me he said, "Mr. Bobbitt, this is an official meeting, so please be honest. Isn't there a chance that you did hit your ball into a bunker but are too embarrassed to admit to having done so?"

"Oh, *man*." I stood up and walked away before I had a chance to say something highly regrettable, such as, "Mister DuPree, please put on a lubricated surgical glove before you give me another finger wave."

While I tried to cool off, DuPree asked some spectators if they had seen anything. When no one said much, he concluded the matter.

"There is inconclusive evidence of an 'outside agency,' so Mister Bobbitt will have to play his ball from where it was discovered in the bunker."

I'd heard enough. "You son of a—"

Everett clapped his hand over my mouth before I had a chance to call DuPree a "retarded sack of shit" or knock him senseless with one of my clubs. After a few minutes of trying to pry my caddy's hand off my face, I began to realize that being convicted of attempted murder and sodomized in prison wasn't quite worth the satisfaction I would get from cracking open the old coot's bean.

Everett then gave me his rap.

"We gonna be better than this, Grover," he murmured. "If they say play it from the bunker, thass what we do. We make the prettiest shot ever and git it in that cup lickety-split. Then we start takin' care of business on the back nine. Thass how we do this thing."

I nodded, accepted my sand wedge from him and stepped down into the bunker. After assuming the best possible stance, I swung as smoothly as I could and hit the ball. I failed; the ball stayed in the bunker.

I frowned at my ball as it lay in the bunker, and I hoped nobody knew that a golf writer had consulted me in his article about extricating oneself from sand traps and even quoted me in his magazine. Gil Donaldo once said that golf magazines and golf instructors were for shitty golfers who wanted to stay that way.

Everett said, "No problems yet, Grover. We can still make this thing work out. Just git it back on the green. The next nine will be easier than this."

I tried it again, and left the ball in the sand.

Everett said, "Pay no mind to nothin'. Just breathe deep and git the ball out. Maybe we double bogey, but thass OK. We got lotta birdies ahead of us and maybe an eagle, too."

I finally got the ball onto the green with my third sand shot. The ball went nowhere near the cup, of course, and I had a forty-foot putt that even Tiger couldn't drop.

Everett said, "Don't mean shit, boss. Ain't nothin' here but golf. Have fun and don't let nothin' git you down."

My first putt went two dozen feet past the cup. My next one came within fifteen feet of the hole. The one after that, seven feet. I then sank that seven-footer. But who cared?

Before the fat bitch got on the course and displaced my ball, and DuPree rejected my appeal, I was on my way to maybe a three or four for that hole. Now I had a nine.

Until the demonstrators and DuPree, I was three or four under and had a half-decent chance of winning this Masters. Now I was two over at 38, completely out of contention. Another big disappointment for Grover Bobbitt, the man who never failed to fail.

As I walked to the 10th tee with Lorna, I sounded matter-of-fact.

"You're off the board," she said. "What's the deal with that?"

"I was a nine on that last hole."

"Nine?" Her eyes bugged out. "How...?"

Everett ran it down for her.

Lorna nodded. "They made you play it from the bunker. That explains it. You must have been really distressed and agitated. I guess you had no recourse."

"No one except Everett stuck up for me." I turned to my caddy. "Say, do you know DuPree's address? We could grab a few clubs and go beat his dead tonight while he sleeps."

19

From then on, everyone played with the utmost seriousness, although some were clearly shaken up by the demonstrators and the chaos they had caused. While I had always had very little use for sportswriters, I felt pleased when they reported that Marni Sandusky and her muckrakers, when swarming over the Masters and wreaking havocs, had merely made perfect fools of themselves and turned their supporters against them. Also, polls indicated that it made those who were undecided about, or indifferent to, the Masters' males-only policy believe that the organization had the right to restrict its membership if it wished to do so.

Tiger Woods, Phil Mickelson and Harris English were the three leaders. I was number four; Everett gave me a pat on the back and a big smile. "You got stick-to-it-iveness, boss. I likes that."

"No big thing," I told him.

Everett shook his head. "No, suh. It take a big man to git hisself together and make a par-thirty-six on the back aftuh havin' to chop his way out of that bunker. You still in fourth place and thass somethin' to be proud about."

I smiled. "Thanks, Everett."

He was wrong, of course. I had played well, but not because of resiliency or tenacity, but out of apathy. I played a loose, careless game, hitting the ball in the general direction of the cup but not really giving a shit where it ended. Despite, or maybe because of, my nonchalance, my balls dropped in more often than not. Hell, I didn't even know I'd gone two under par until Everett told me so.

I knew why Everett smiled about my fourth-place finish. It meant he would receive tens of thousands of dollars, his share of my purse. But he was happy for other reasons. He liked me even when I made myself very hard to like. He felt glad that I had done moderately well and pocketed a couple of hundred thousand dollars for my effort. If I had choked, fucked up and humiliated myself, it wouldn't have surprised him in the least.

Andy Warhol had said, "In the future, everyone will be famous for fifteen minutes." He might have added, "Grover Bobbitt will lead the Masters for exactly that long." He would have been right.

For that reason, I ended up in the press room, that place where they usually had no use for me. I sat at the table, a live microphone before me, a couple of green-jacketed old men on each side of me. Only half a dozen reports considered me worthy of their time. Most of their colleagues were out on the course, trying to predict the winner and cheering for that person. All of those media folks wanted to avoid a sudden-death situation that would prolong the contest into the evening and require everyone to return the following day.

One of the old men said to nobody in particular, "Here we have the current Masters leader."

This, of course, happened before DuPree and some

demonstrator conspired to destroy my soul. The reporters, displaying a remarkable ignorance of me, asked me how to spell my name. I told them about my Canadian roots, three ex-wives and zero major wins, believing that they wanted to hear such things. Apparently they did, because they wrote it down as soon as I said it.

Later on, Clark Irving took me aside and said, "I really hope you win this thing, if only because it will appeal to my readers from so many angles—forty years old, first major, a Canadian. Frankly, I'm tired of writing, 'Tiger's got so many green jackets, he could open his own store by now.'"

"Maybe," I said, "I could steal one when he's not looking."

Gil Donaldo sat sipping something that looked yummy when I entered the players' lounge. I sat down with him and said, "Congratulations, guy. You're tied for eighth."

He nodded. "And no bunkers or idiot officials to trip me up."

We watched the TV monitor. Tiger stood there, pumping his fist.

Gil pointed to the glass of Canadian Comfort over ice that had been placed where I sat. "That's for you. Wish it could be a trophy, but you get what you get."

"Snead, Palmer, Nicklaus," I said, "could have gone through what happened to me—the idiot official making me play from the bunker—and those guys still would have won this tournament. Fuck!"

I took a big gulp of Canadian Comfort and had to

wait a minute or two for the fire in my chest to subside.

Gil said, "Run it down for me, Grover. TV just shows the fat women whooping and hollering all over the course, carrying on like six-year-olds."

I told him about the official named Morrison Weatherby DuPree or something, the ugly old Mayflower prick who'd probably gone to Rice or Duke and thought he was American gentry. Then I went on for a bit about my epic battle to rescue my ball from the bunker.

Gil shook his head and said, "Nasty."

"'Nasty' doesn't touch it. Try 'fucked in the ass.'"

"What did you say the coot's name was?"

"Morrison Weatherby DuPree."

"Well, Grover, it could have been worse."

"How you figure that?"

"He could have been a fag with a crush on you," Gil said.

We both burst out laughing.

Both us of sat still for a moment and watched as Tiger Woods, surrounded by men in green jackets, received his latest green jacket. He smiled and shook hands, looking entirely too pleased with himself.

"Gil," I asked, "did Tiger fuck up at all?"

He smiled and shook his head. "Naw, he just played clean golf again. Phil and a few of the others landed in the water on fifteen but Tiger birdied. He probably knew then that he would win this thing."

"Did they say anything on TV about the protestors? Anyone get busted?"

"The Masters chairman said that nobody, including Marni Sandusky, would be arrested," Gil told me. "Still, he hoped that they would realize that their actions were useless and immoral. The Masters would try to find out if anyone had sold illegal passes, and those people would be barred for life."

"Where's the Prick?"

"Oh, he hauled ass a long time ago. He lives up to his nickname. What a fucking whiner! He goes on an on whenever things don't go his way."

"Lance Priklan got an attitude at the Masters, eh?"

"Sure did. His putts were a big problem. Well, shit, this is the Masters, it's one of the world's most challenging courses, so, yeah, you're probably going to struggle with your putts, especially when it's your first time here. But he's like, 'I'm Lance Priklan, King Shit of Golf, I'm supposed to make my putts.' So King Shit throws a temper tantrum in the locker room, blaming everyone but the Man in the Moon for his golf troubles. Then he stalks off and doesn't even tip the attendant like he's supposed to. That kid needs to grow up."

"I don't think you can give an attitude adjustment to a twenty-year-old who can already buy and sell you thirty times over. Did you say anything to him about it when he was acting out?"

"No way. He's twice my size. He'd kick my ass," said Gil.

I had one last dinner with Lorna Priklan. We ate in her room because we no longer needed to worry that Lance would start banging on her door. He had thrown his clubs into his trunk, fired up his Beemer or Porsche and zoomed off.

People who have regular cars can get from Georgia to Florida in probably eight hours, depending on how many meal and toilet breaks they take. Lance would get there in about six. I guessed he would be at home, being laid by one of his honeys, before midnight. He'd have enough sense to own a radar detector, so the cops wouldn't pull him over and write him up.

So Lorna and I got into our birthday suits and did those things that lovers did. We did them before and after dinner, and then we lay in a sweaty, smelly heap, too tired to do anything but fall into a very long, deep sleep.

In the morning, we ate a big, filling breakfast on her balcony. I had signed up for a tournament in Hawaii; Lorna was going back home to California. A local bus would transport her to Hartsfield Airport, where she would catch a direct flight to LAX.

"What do we do now?" she asked, finishing her coffee.

"Excuse me?"

"I mean, we met here, and I watched while you played. Now I'm going to California and you're off to Hawaii. So…what now?"

"Well," I said, "we play telephone tag for a little while, then we make remarkably inconvenient and expensive plans to meet up just for the sake of being together. You OK with that?"

She smiled. "Sounds like a plan."

PART TWO

20

On the evening before the U.S. Open began, Lorna and I enjoyed a stroll through the streets of Pinehurst, being amused and charmed but thinking that there were other places just as lovely. We had eaten at the Tar Heel Inn, an old favorite of mine; Lorna had chosen to stay there. The inn's restaurant had plenty of greenery to provide ambience, yet it didn't make us feel as if we were eating in a forest. The place had a great bar, too—if I had been there alone, I would have tried to pick up some Southern belle for the night.

I'd wanted to stay with Lorna at the Tar Heel Inn, to ravish her each night and wake up with her in my arms. But how would it have looked? Besides, this was the second major of the year, and I needed no distractions, so I'd registered at the Pine Valley Inn, a lovingly restored mansion a few hundred yards from the Tar Heel.

For that week, the Pine Valley Inn belonged to the USGA, which booked its officials in there. It also housed whichever players could afford the place. Gil Donaldo and Jake Grimsley were there, as well as Lance Priklan and most of the famous golfers.

Those who stayed at the Pine Valley, Tar Heel or Cedarway didn't have the hassles of security guards or vehicular traffic. The second-class citizens—reporters, golfers too frugal or stingy to stay at the better places, and most of the fans—made do at highway motels.

Lorna and I walked arm in arm through the quaint little village. "I like North Carolina as much as anywhere else I've ever been to. Of course, I'm from Canada, so it would be too hot for me to live here."

"Dixie," Lorna said. "Look away, look away…"

I laughed. "Yeah, we're back in Dixieland. I don't know that it's still cotton-and-tobacco turf, though. Seems like it's all about golf now. To a foreigner like me, all Americans are called Yankees. But to people down here, Yankees are people from the northern United States."

"Gee," Lorna said, "I thought the Civil War had ended."

I laughed. "Well, you can't believe everything you read. Ulysses Grant and Robert Lee had some different views on things, like slavery, but they were both cold-blooded killers."

"Grant won the war, didn't he?"

"Yankees seem to think so."

"I wonder what would have happened if the Confederates had won."

"This country would be a *very* different place today," I said.

"Two countries instead of one," Lorna said.

"Actually, four or five countries. Texas would be a sovereign country, and so would California and Utah."

"California, too? Hard to believe."

"The Dakotas, Montana, Wyoming, Colorado and Oregon would have comprised one country, but that country would have failed and become American states during the Great Depression. Abe Lincoln wouldn't have been assassinated."

"Why not?"

"Because Booth wouldn't have had any reason to kill him."

"Talk about altering history," Lorna said.

"Jefferson Davis would have been the Confederate president. Robert Lee would have been his special envoy to the United States."

"You don't say."

"It gets better. The countries that are now known as America would have stayed out of World War One," I said.

"Hard to imagine. Without Uncle Sam, that war would have gone on for much longer."

"Yes, ma'am. Slavery would have lasted until Nineteen-twenty."

"Really?" Lorna asked. "Why would it have ended?"

"Because it would have outlasted its usefulness. But racial integration would have continued, anyway, which would have been a big issue no matter what had happened."

"And that's still going on." Then, "What about World War Two? Would we have stayed out of that, too?"

I shook my head. "The American countries would have formed some sort of alliance to fight the Nazis. But each country would have sent its own leader to fight Germany and Japan, and when the war was over the American countries would have remained separate entities, like America and Canada—getting along most of the time, but bitching at one another about economic and political matters."

"We have such a colorful history in this country," Lorna said, sighing. "Too bad we don't appreciate it that much. I mean, you're a Canadian but you've already forgotten more about American history than I've ever learned."

"Maybe," I said, "that's because Canadian history is so boring." I added, "But returning to the present day.

Pinehurst here is all about golf, nothing else. These people really are hardcore golf junkies."

"But it has nice art galleries, too. Grover, why do you like it so much? Lance has played here and says it's awful."

"Lance doesn't seem to like much of anyone or anything. He'll love it once he wins a few tournaments here. This place is different, and I mean that in a good way. No out-of-bounds areas or water hazards. Its challenges are subtle. You have to be very patient."

"Lance isn't known for his patience," Lorna muttered.

"They have rolling fairways here. The greens overwhelm you. A guy can spend all day trying to get off the fairway and onto the green. Even the best pros can get exasperated."

"You have the patience and experience," Lorna said. "If you're ever going to win that major, this is the right course for you."

"Maybe."

She chuckled. "Just 'maybe'?"

I shrugged. "I'm not legendary for making birdies or eagles. My putting has always been a problem. Around here, just making par is something to be proud of. These greens have quite an attitude. Plus, I'm no kid anymore."

"I wish you were a bit more optimistic," she said. "I hope that teenaged girl won't be an issue for you."

Lorna meant Hana Palmer, the statuesque, voluptuous fifteen-year-old cutie who had captivated the golf world for most of the past year. The USGA, in a moment of insanity, had invited her to participate in the Open.

I scratched my head. "A teenaged girl in a men's golf

tournament? Am I the only one who's thinking, *What the fuck?*"

"It's weird," said Lorna. "Probably everyone here is laughing about it or angry. And I'm sure Hana knows it."

"How would she like it if *I* played in the Fifteen Year Old Girls' Open?"

Lorna laughed. "Is there such a tournament?"

"No, but maybe we should invent one so that I could insist on playing in it."

"Then we would have Marni Sandusky out there, saying, 'This is for teenaged girls, not old men.'"

"Yeah," I said, "then I could get Gil Donaldo, Jake Grimsley, Stu Claudell and a bunch of the other guys to invade the tour and stomp all over the greens like Marni's bunch did."

"What if you picked up the leader's ball and chucked into the sand? Then the official made her play from the bunker, like they did to you. How do you think *she* would feel?"

I laughed. "I think the girl whose ball I threw into the bunker would burst into tears and the official would say, 'There, there, dear. Where would you like to put your ball?' What happened to *me* could never happen to anyone else. I was put in this world to have shit happen to me."

"We won't talk about that right now," Lorna said. "If you could afford it, where would you, as a golfer, choose to live? Here? It *is* quaint."

"I would choose Pebble Beach. Seventeen Mile Drive. Out your way. Clint Eastwood owns a house there. I took a tour through there once. The diver said, 'There's Clint's house.' I'm like, 'Wow! Let's knock on his door, see if he'll have us in for a coffee.' Then the driver said, 'There's Gene Hackman's house.' I thought, 'Hmm, I didn't know that Gene Hackman could afford to buy into a neighborhood like this.'"

"Eastwood bought into that part of the world many years ago, when it was less expensive than it is today," Lorna said. "Also, he owns the Malpaso Company, which produces his movies, and his movies always make money, thus his wealth."

"If you lived on Seventeen Mile Drive," Lorna told me, "you would just golf, golf, golf at Pebble Beach. You would never get anything else done."

"Something wrong with that?"

We both laughed.

"Actually," she said, "you couldn't live there because your house would be too big. You would get lost in there. Or, because you don't cook, you would get lost on your way to get something to eat."

"Then maybe I'll just stay in Canada," I said.

We stopped walking and looked into the window of a gift shop. Most of the items seemed to be made of cut glass or some other dainty, fine material, and everything seemed to be a golf ball or club or golfer.

"See? I told you that place cared only about golf," I said.

"I can't imagine what their prices are."

"You don't want to know," I told her.

"Too right."

"Everything is what it is," I said. "Except when it isn't."

"That's so profound," Lorna said. "*You're* so profound."

"I wish I could claim credit for that observation, but I think Socrates or Descartes or maybe Sartre said it first."

"Well, I'm going to repeat it and claim it as my own original thought," she said.

"Knock yourself out," I replied.

21

Hana Palmer, five feet ten, could stand at her tee and drive her ball twenty yards farther than most of the men. She could make a man look like a fifteen-year-old girl, which was not altogether a good thing.

"Check her out," I muttered to Lorna as we watched Hana whack her ball into the vast sky. The woman-child, or child-woman, did so with little discernible effort.

We sat outdoors, enjoying the balmy Southern day. We had walked around the village, then loitered in the huge clubhouse, and ended up outside so Lorna could smoke a Newport.

I sat there and gazed at that teenaged golfer, trying to decide if I thought she was pretty or plain. She had shapely legs, a heart-shaped bum and a decent pair of zoomers. She also had a clear complexion, rosy cheeks and a big, open smile. Still, there was something about her that was a bit too sturdy and masculine for me.

I saw nothing immoral about getting an erection in my pants while ogling a fifteen-year-old girl. I also would have felt perfectly OK about getting a hard-on while looking at a fifteen-year-old boy, if I'd liked males that way.

Standing near Hana, a skinny, sneering man with his arms folded and head shaking.

"Who's that guy?" asked Lorna.

"Mason Palmer, Hana's daddy."

Mason, heir to the Palmer enterprises fortune in

New England, had started out life as a fat, pimply kid with a spectacular overbite. Through orthodontia, fat farms and many visits to his dermatologist, he had overcome his cosmetic deficits but still felt compelled to get facelifts and hair transplants and endure excruciating diets. He also bought the most expensive clothing available but often mismatched them. His face looked too tightly stretched; his too-abundant hair sat across his skull in uneven patterns.

Hana's mum, I'd heard, obsessed over her daughter's media coverage and had complied many computer files of the stories written about the adolescent golfer.

"In their family," I muttered to Lorna, "it's all about Hana and her golfing."

She made a face. "Maybe we should introduce her to Lance. We could be one huge dysfunctional family."

"Lance would get busted for being with a fifteen-year-old."

Lorna nodded. "Then maybe we won't introduce them."

"Good call."

Although born in Massachusetts, Hana, according to the online news services, had spent most of her life since age eight or so down in Florida, at some golf camp that doubled as a boarding school.

"I've read plenty about her," I told Lorna. "When she was at that golf camp? She took on the best of America's other girl golfers her age and sent them home crying to Mummy."

"I don't doubt it. She's got the build and coordination for all kinds of sports. I wonder if she plays tennis. She sort of reminds me of Martina or Billie Jean."

"Or Ivan Lendl with tits," I said.

"I hope she's not another Marni Sandusky," Lorna muttered. "Life is hard enough when you're, you know, normal. Hana looks a bit butch, but I really hope she's straight."

"Me, too. Hana is just the latest of girlie golfers who can beat the guys. Annika Sorenstam and Michelle Wie started the whole thing. Hana has already gone up against the guys a few times."

"How'd she do?"

"She made the cut each time. Finished in the top twenty. Beat Gil Donaldo and Jake Grimsley. I said, 'I can't believe a fifteen-year-old girl beat you!'"

"What did *they* say?"

"They said, '*You* try playing against her, asshole!'"

"She sounds like Lance," Lorna said. "I wonder if she throws tantrums like he does."

"No, her daddy does it for her," I retorted. "She just goes out there and *does it*. Sets up her tee ball, swings her driver and whammo!—off it goes. I hear she's got quite a short game, too."

"Can you beat this chick?" Lorna asked me.

"Ask me something else."

How Hana got to the Open at Pinehurst was an easy story to learn if one kept his ears open and already knew how much the USGA craved greenbacks.

The USGA didn't always love money so much, of course. It just wanted to run its tournaments and be able to pay all of its bills. But then it saw how some dummies were making piles of cash, and the USGA said, "Let's git us some of dat!"

The USGA did away with some of their honorable traditions and said to the TV networks and corporate sponsors, "We want to sell you our soul."

Their avarice led them to Mason Palmer, who owned DataServ, a company that made inferior software, and ChemCo, whose products were of use mostly to crystal-meth chefs.

DataServ and ChemCo bought the two largest corporate hospitality tents at Pinehurst's Open. Then Mason bought some more USGA friendship. His total investment in the Open was around $20 million.

"So, after that," I told Lorna as she stubbed out her Newport, "Mason asked for a teensy little favor in return for his remarkable largesse."

"'Let my daughter play'?" Lorna asked. "In the men's Open."

I nodded. "And the USGA, naturally, thought he was kidding. They call it the men's Open for a reason. The current president, Sid James, said something like, 'No can do, and I'm offended that you'd ask.'"

"So Mason probably threatened to take back what he'd given them. Those tents, all that money…"

"Yeah, and they said, 'Mason, you can't do that.' And Mason said, 'Oh, can't I? Watch me try.' So Sid makes the mistake of saying to someone, 'Mason's such a doofus,' and it gets back to Mason. Mason says, 'I'm going to buy Sid's worthless ass and make sure he spends the rest of his life sleeping in alleyways.'"

"Did they take Mason's threats seriously?"

"Damn right. You don't fuck around with rich people because they have the resources to hurt you. So Mason's flexing some heavy muscle and the USGA bosses are convening in a meeting room, and they emerge all smiles. They say, 'We have made a special exemption for Hana Palmer to play in the Open.'"

"That's a nasty, tasty story," Lorna said. "Was it all online, for everyone to read?"

"No, just some of it. I found out the rest because I knew the right people and they have big mouths."

"Plus, you're a good listener. Anyway, I think it'll be fun to see how Hana does in this tournament."

"It could be even better," I said.

"Really? How?"

"Instead of Hana, we could be playing against Marni Sandusky."

"Funny guy."

22

Since meeting Lorna at the Masters, she had been my top priority in life. I had missed five of the nine golf events between the Masters and the Open in Pinehurst. While the other guys were hitting balls and making money, I'd been flying to California to shack up with Lorna or playing house with her in Bayporte.

I had shown up for La Costa, however. I knew the course and the town well. But when I hooked up with Lorna, she treated me like a wide-eyed tourist eager to snap at surfers and beach babes with his iPhone.

"See that mass of blue?" Lorna asked me. "It's called the Pacific Ocean. See that tender young thing with almost nothing on? She's called a California beach girl."

"Yeah," I retorted. "We have stuff like that up in Canada."

Lorna pointed out the skinny women doing their shopping and having lunch in La Jolla as we sat sipping cocktails in a pink-painted hotel. Been there, done that...a few times. They had preserved the town so that it looked like a Forties movie set. Well, I had to admit, they didn't have stuff like La Jolla up in Canada.

I thought that Lorna's Carmel art gallery, the Creative Condition, would do well in La Jolla. She had taken me in and introduced me to the two Julia Roberts lookalikes who worked for her. Katie Sanford, the co-owner, a petite blonde with big zoomers, shook my hand and said to Lorna, "He's *much* better than that joker you married."

"Keep your hands off," Lorna said.

"Bitch." Both women laughed.

I felt pleased that Lorna's house up was a simple yet spacious Spanish-style split-level abode. No fake waterfalls or other ostentatious bullshit.

She kept some of Lance's medals and trophies in her living room. His tall silver replica of the U.S. Amateur trophy fairly dominated room. She had placed his other trophies here and there, and his medals sat in a mahogany-and-glass case she'd had built just for that purpose. My mum would have done the same thing, if I'd won anything worth displaying.

"He's won more than all this," she said. "Some of it is with Bruce, his dad, who manages him and a few other athletes."

"I'm surprised Lance doesn't have any of this on display in Florida," I said.

"Right now, the trophies he likes are two-legged females and four-wheeled vehicles."

"Does Bruce have any clients I might know?" I asked her.

Lorna shrugged. "He keeps mum about that stuff, you know. I think he's after a couple of teenaged girls who are coming up in tennis and skiing. He thinks he could make a few bucks off them. Lance said his dad is chasing down a couple of 'top secret' deals."

I remember Lorna's house as a place where the bedroom was big and beautiful.

When Lorna visited Bayporte, I did my usual thing when entertaining friends who were new to my city. I drove her all over, complained about the rain and the outrageous cost of everything. When they asked why I persisted in residing here, I told them that it was the only home I'd ever known.

"The skyscrapers," Lorna pointed out, "all look about fifteen minutes old."

"That's the Canadian way," I told her. "Once it starts to age, knock it down and replace it with something new."

"American tourists probably come up here expecting log cabins and people killing their food and cooking it outdoors," Lorna paused. "This is all shiny and new. I'm not sure if that's good or bad."

"If you're looking for log cabins and that whole rustic rugged outdoorsy thing," I told her, "Canada still has plenty of that. You just have to look for it."

Lorna laughed. "I'm not looking for it, thank you very much. I enjoy sleeping in a bed and having my breakfast served to me."

I took her to Panache, Bayporte's closest thing to a restaurant with an international reputation. There we ate Pacific salmon and drank Canadian white wine. Later we held hands and strolled through that brick-paved, tree-lined labyrinth called Northup University, and I felt really awkward bragging about it to a Stanford alumna.

"It's mostly an engineering school," I told her. "They've made huge cuts in all the other departments. The surrounding neighborhood is so expensive that most of the professors can't afford to live out this way."

"Yeah, I saw all those mansions as we drove in. Still, a very pretty campus. I can see why kids from all over Canada come to study here."

"It's pretty because it's sunny today. If it were

raining like mad, as it often does, the campus would gray and dreary. I spent four years here, majoring in smoking weed, drinking beer and playing golf."

"Time well spent. Did the rain get you down? It's better than snow," she said.

"Been in the snow much?" I asked her.

"A few times, and I really hated it."

"I don't like the white stuff so much myself."

I made sure I took her to Paul's Submarine Sandwich Stop, my favorite place in the whole world.

"What's the big deal?" Lorna asked as I escorted her in. "Submarine sandwiches? You're such a cheap date! Maybe I won't put out for you tonight."

"Just wait. You'll love it."

We sat down.

"I went to high school just down the street at a place called Oliver Johnson High. We all used to eat here every day. Best sandwiches in the world."

"You would think it was Saigon or New Delhi, judging from the signs outside," she said.

"Yeah, it's been that way for a few years," I said, walking away to get our sandwiches. Presently I returned with two steaming steak-and-onion subs.

"Mmmm! Smells wonderful!" Lorna took a bite and closed her eyes.

I smiled. "They've been this good since I was a kid."

"Why don't the Subway and other chains make them this good?"

"Because," I told her, "it's a big fuckin' hassle. You need the best ingredients and you have to fry it all on the griddle. You also gotta toast the bread on the griddle. Only *then* do you have an authentic Paul's sandwich."

I took her through our art museums, which

impressed her not at all. We caught a Nickelback concert at Great Elizabeth Place, where the Invaders had won the first all-Canadian Super Bowl a few years earlier against the Toronto Stars. We went dancing at the Igloo, Bayporte's oldest and most famous nightclub.

We hung out for a while at Placid Oaks, the city's most exclusive golf course and country club. "Tiger loves this place. He comes up here to play as often as he can," I told her.

"What does he play? And with whom?"

"Golf," I told her. "He plays golf, with other golfers."

"I see," she said.

That evening, we had dinner with my parents, so they could get a good look at her and decide if they liked her or not.

23

I needed to explain some things to Lorna so that Margaret and Arthur Bobbitt wouldn't totally freak her out. I said that my mum was a good-natured older woman who liked to play bingo, sing songs and smoke cigarettes. My dad, I explained, was the fairly handsome old guy who really wasn't nearly as crabby as he appeared to be. He loved to drink beer, play cards and use profanity. He also used to love fucking women he wasn't married to, but age and an enlarged prostate had ended his infidelity.

As soon as I introduced Lorna to my folks, my dad said, "She's the prettiest one yet. He's sure brought a lot of ugly ones around. He's married a few losers, you know."

Lorna nodded, not knowing what else to do.

My mum served us a salad, followed by ham, black beans and cornbread. There were no greens on anyone's plate. My dad believed that salads and vegetables were for poor people. He'd throw a temper tantrum served such foods. She, and their doctor, wanted him to eat roughage, but it wasn't worth the trouble of getting the old boy angry.

"It's all too yummy," Lorna said. "Especially this cornbread. So moist and fluffy."

"It's called 'home cookin'," said my dad. "People don't know that is. They think McDonald's and Taco Bell serve food. They don't. They serve empty calories."

We spoke of many things that evening.

Dad said how much he liked the security gates they

had recently installed at Placid Oaks. "I didn't think I would like the gates, but they look fine. Got to keep the riff raff out, you know."

"Do gates really provide protection?" Lorna asked. "What if you don't live in a gated community?"

Dad glowered at her. "Then buy a gun."

"That's funny," said Lorna, "coming from a Canadian. I thought you people hated guns. I thought the attitude up here was, 'Let the police carry the guns so the average Joe and Jane don't have to.'"

"Well," Dad said, "sometimes the police aren't there when you need them. And when they *are* there, they make things worse."

Mum said, "I've loved going to the movies all my life. I still do, except for the ones where they drop an F-bomb every ten seconds."

Lorna giggled. "Well, that's most movies today, isn't it?"

Dad said, "You couldn't get me into a movie house today no matter what. I stopped going when they stopped putting butter or margarine on the popcorn. You know what they use now? Butter-flavored vegetable oil. Isn't that the most disgusting thing you've ever heard?"

Lorna shrugged. "I guess it's cheaper for the theatre to use vegetable oil instead of butter."

Dad nodded. "That's exactly why they do it. But don't they understand how much it offends their customers?" He added, "There was a movie theatre here in downtown Bayporte. They opened it in something like Nineteen Sixty-five and called it the Imperial Six. Well, it was there for so many years and the lease expired or something, so they decided to close the theatre. You know what? For the last few months of the Imperial's life, they pulled the plug: No more maintenance of any kind. The Imperial had always been a place that looked and smelled great. But now, the carpeting was filthy and the place reeked of cigarette smoke. Half the seats were broken and they didn't fix them. But they sure charged full price for tickets and popcorn while they let the place rot."

Lorna shrugged. "Business as usual."

Dad said, "Hey, Grover, you got a good listener here. Keep her for those days when your golf game sucks."

I nodded. "Father knows best."

My parents were comfortable retirees. They had sold their gas station/convenience store business, which they had operated with much success for many years. They had success because they worked hard. Dad now spent most of his time playing golf, with lots of mulligans, and getting angry at the "idiots and assholes" who owned the Bayporte Invaders, Bullies and Rainmakers as well as the "wimps and pussies" who played for those teams.

"If the Northup Kodiaks don't get it together and find a better quarterback," Dad said, "they'll give me a coronary faster than all the TV networks put together."

I said to Lorna, "My dad has this thing about yelling instructions to the players and coaches on TV and then getting mad because they don't pay any attention to him."

"And then he gets chest pains?" asked Lorna.

"That he do," Dad said.

"Lorna," Mum said, "I need a nicotine fix. Let's step outside."

The two women lit up. Dad loved his cigarettes as much as Mum did, but his cardiologist said, "Smoke or breathe—it's up to you." So Mum kept on with hers, often blowing her secondhand smoke into Dad's face.

"I'll tell you what I hate," my father said to Lorna. "I hate terrorists. I felt that way long before Nine-eleven. They're all cowards. They don't deserve to live. But what confuses me is how so many people think the War on Terrorism can be won with love. Hugs and handshakes and smiles and kisses? Come on! The only thing terrorists understand is being killed. We didn't start this war, but we don't have the option of failing to win it. What's your political affiliation?"

"Libertarian," Lorna said.

"How do you feel about flag burners?"

Lorna shrugged. "It's a publicity stunt. They do it when the TV cameras are around."

"Flag burning oughta be legal," Dad said.

"Really?" Lorna asked, frowning.

"Yes. But the beating the dumb bastard receives also oughta be legal."

"My dad was a bit young for World War Two," I said, "but he served in the Royal Canadian Army."

"I didn't go to war," Dad said. "They stationed me in parts of Canada. I'm glad Canada didn't send people to Vietnam. That was an ugly thing."

"He talks like *such* a patriot," Mum said, "but did you notice our cars outside? A Honda and a Toyota. Our TV is a Sony. Our computer is a Toshiba."

"Damn right. I'm not going to apologize for that. Those Nips make damn good products."

"So you served but didn't go overseas," Lorna said. "What *did* you do in the military?"

"Mainly," Dad said, "I kept my mouth shut and freezed my nuts off."

Lorna hooted.

"Kind of wished I *had* gone overseas and wasted some gooks. Then I would have some stories to tell and things to brag about. You a political animal, Lorna?"

She thought for a moment. "I vote, if that's what you mean. But the people who run for office? It's like they're just blowing sunshine up our asses: 'If you vote for me, I'll do this and that for you.' Blah, blah, blah. When Arnold Schwarzenegger became governor, he basically promised everything to everyone. I know he meant well and worked hard, but he just couldn't deliver on all those promises. So after he left office, people were saying, 'He was a bad governor.'"

"Who said that?" Dad asked.

"Democrats," Lorna replied.

"You know what kind of people become Democrats?"

Lorna smiled. "Tell me."

"People who don't have any hobbies."

"And people who don't get laid often enough," Lorna retorted.

"Them too," Dad said, and they both laughed.

It took a special kind of woman to make my father laugh, and I considered our evening a triumph.

24

My three ex-wives were not lazy people. They all had full-time jobs and liked to hang out at the same Bayporte places that I went to. If they had been less busy, Lorna and I would have seen them during our walks about town.

Alicia Theodore still worked for that criminal lawyer, Tad Reddert, so she spent her eight hours each day in his musty old office, doing good things for bad people. She kept her sense of humor. "Who says crime doesn't pay?"

Tad had represented 2 Kool 4 Skool, the infamously profane rapper who, due to illiteracy, composed his tunes into his cell phone.

While chillin' at Bayporte International Airport on his way to LAX, Kool found out that his flight to California would be delayed by weather. He decided to kill some time by working on a new song as he stood with the other passengers at his gate. Kool began rapping into his iPhone, loudly and fairly intelligibly, and soon began drawing inspiration from Muriel Kendrick, a septuagenarian also waiting for the flight. Kool, his iPhone an inch from his lips, walked up to Muriel, his right index finger pointed at her, and rapped about an "old bitch-ass white cunt." He said plenty more, and, possibly for emphasis, squeezed the sizable bulge in his pants. But red-faced Muriel, having heard quite enough, thank you, tried to shoo him away by poking him in the package with her cane. That was when 2 Kool 4 Skool lost it. He hauled out his snub-nosed .38 and shot Muriel Kendrick in the face.

Kool called Tad for help, and Tad entered a plea of self-defense on Kool's behalf. He told Alicia to pay a couple of crackheads to claim they were there and had seen the whole thing go down. They testified that the old woman had tried to "permanently disable" the buff, six-foot rapper by assaulting him where it *really* hurt, and he, wounded and humiliated, did the only thing he could—took out his piece and popped her. The jury took fifteen minutes to set him free.

"Today, a fine young man got justice," Tad told the media. "Now he can go home to Los Angeles and resume his distinguished entertainment career. We all hope he can put this awful incident behind him."

Later, Alicia assisted Tad in a real estate deal that involved some of the murderers, rapists and armed robbers he had gotten acquitted.

The city needed to relocate a couple of hundred criminals from Bayporte Towers, a crumbling housing project in the seediest part of downtown. The city had just sold Bayporte Towers to a developer who wanted to replace the towers with "microloft" highrises that would be 250 square feet per unit and rent for nearly a thousand dollars per month.

Tad, a friend of some of the board members, advised them to buy the Excelsior, an apartment building located near West Shore. All of the Excelsior's suites had two bedrooms, TVs, computers, fireplaces and a big swimming pool.

Loud, livid public hearings occurred over the possible move of criminals into the Excelsior. Homeowners near the building said they would fear for their lives and the resale value of their homes.

At one of the hearings, Alicia pretended to be an Excelsior resident. "Canada is the home of the second chances," she said at the microphone. "All of those men just need some help, patience and kindness to get their lives back together. We'll be glad we did."

The homeowners got the felons as their new neighbors, even if they weren't glad to have them. Soon after the convicts' relocation into the Excelsior began, news reports said that Tad Reddert was a part owner of the Excelsior and the city had bought the building for close to $60 million.

The Bayporter received countless emails that mostly said, "One day, people like Tad Reddert will no longer be here, and this city will be a better place because of it."

Alicia Theodore told me, "Grover, I had never seen such sorry sons of bitches as those felons who got moved from the project into the Excelsior. They'll destroy that place within a year."

"Then why did you go to that meeting and beg the homeowners to welcome the felons?"

She shrugged. "Because Tad asked me to."

Helene Chernays surely stayed busy with her charitable work and socialite activities. I didn't know about her job as an exclusive realtor, selling mansions to the few who could afford them. In Bayporte, the richest people were Chinese emigrants from Hong Kong who insisted on buying their mansions and cars from other Chinese people. I guessed that she filled her days with Variety Club and Bayporte Philharmonic meetings. She had doubtless become an expert on the kinds of white wine to serve with dainty sandwiches.

No longer the Helene I had known, the cute, sassy, trailer-trash chick who wore low-cut tops to show off her pushed-up zoomers. She used to joyride through town in her VW convertible with the top down, weaving in and out of traffic, missing other vehicles by inches as drivers honked at her. She'd put on a bumper sticker that said I JUST BROKE UP WITH YOUR MAN.

One day Helene left a message on my answering machine. Lorna heard it and laughed.

"Hey, dickless, this is Miss Phoney Baloney," Helene said. "Who are you to call me names? Some friends told me they had seen you around and you asked, 'How's Miss Phoney Baloney doing?' Last time I checked, your parents had spent their lives running a gas station, and you're forty years old who calls himself a pro golfer even though you've never won a major, so who the fuck do you think you are, making fun of me and my lifestyle? How about *you* stay on *your* half of the city and *I'll* stay on *mine*?"

"So, that was my ex," I said to Lorna. "What did you think?"

Lorna shrugged. "What can I say? She's just another class broad."

Simone Allerd, my favorite ex-wife, still one of my best friends and business partner, continued to run Afternoon Delights, the popular candy store near the Northup University campus. I wanted her to meet

Lorna, if only to prove to my new lady that I had at least one woman friend who wasn't a cunt.

But Simone's assistant said that the boss that stepped out just minutes before.

"Simone's gone to deliver a bunch of truffles to a party some rich people are having," the assistant said.

"How come only rich people eat truffles?" I asked.

The assistant shrugged. "Because they're so expensive?"

25

When I wasn't hanging out and goofing off with Lorna, I rejoined the Tour and golfed all over the States. My weeks at a time with Lorna, and without golf, weakened my game and seldom did I play well enough for my name to appear on the leader board. However, many others played even worse than I did, so I usually managed to pocket my share of scratch.

Scratch was Gil Donaldo's word for prize money.

"You gotta have the scratch to get the snatch," Gil liked to say, his version of the saying, "You gotta get paid if you wanna get laid."

"You can get some serious scratch," he might also say, "if your rod don't get scoliosis." By rod, he meant putter; and by scoliosis, he meant that sometimes the putter acted as if it were curved.

I believed that putters were the most temperamental pieces of golf equipment. Often I found myself unable to speak to mine with any civility, and feared at times that would take it across my thigh and snap it in half.

Gil Doanldo told me that every putter that ever existed, if given enough time, would turn on its owner and do its best to undermine his game.

"Putters are evil," he's said. "They can't help it. That's just the way they are."

I disappointed my fellow Bayporters at Placid Oaks,

too. I tried too hard to dazzle my fans and my score stayed above par. Still, I received a very nice check for one hundred, sixty-five thousand dollars, my reward for finishing tied for twelfth or wherever I placed.

I had psyched myself out by worrying if Lance Priklan would like Bayporte and Placid Oaks. I shouldn't have fretted. On his first night, I took him to Wong's, my favorite Chinese buffet. He cleaned his plate three times and drank down six tall iced teas.

"This tea is sweet," he said, looking sour. "Don't they have unsweetened iced tea?"

I shook my head. "This is Canada, Lance. They don't know that unsweetened iced tea exists."

I also needn't have worried about how a handsome young celebrity like Lance Priklan would find a good time in Bayporte. The good time would find *him*.

His good times happened courtesy of dental assistants, paralegals, receptionists and a few other local ladies who wished to make sure that Lance didn't get lonely.

"I love this town!" he exclaimed between seductions. His new friends hadn't tuckered him out completely; he won the Placid Oaks tournament by half a dozen strokes.

Lorna, calling from California, thanked me for being such a great host to Lance.

"It was nothing," I said, meaning that almost literally. I introduced him to some ladies; they did the rest.

"I was kind of surprised that he shot so well," Lorna said. "On TV, he kept yawning. I thought he would fall asleep."

"He did look a bit tired. I guess he partied and had some late nights," I told her.

I played at Memphis and Nashville and New Orleans. I finished ninth here and fifteenth there, and Gil Donaldo played well more often than not. But the big event for us was a visit with Barney Smoltz, our agent, who arrived at our hotel in Memphis. Gil, Barney and I walked down Beale Street for a plateful of hot, fattening, wonderful cuisine.

"This is the stuff that killed Elvis," Barney said. "Damn, it tastes good." Then he gave us a business proposal.

He had been in touch with a Fort Worth, Texas, company called Golf Buddy, which made a product called Cool It, a padded cup that a golfer would put his beer bottle or coffee cup into so that the beverage would stay cold or hot. Gil and I would become part owners of Golf Buddy if we agreed to become the "Golf Buddies" who appeared in ads.

"Did you know," Gil said, "that some golfers make millions just by wearing a company's cap or shirt?"

Barney shrugged. "Well, some golfers have won major tournaments."

"Ouch," I said.

Gil said, "Barney, when I finish this plate of food, do you wanna know what I'm gonna do? I'm gonna drop a big smelly deuce into your Cool It cup."

Gil and I drove together to the Houston tournament in

his Hummer. We'd preferred to drive after 9/11, when air travel, due to the inconvenience and paranoia, had become a sort of last resort to us. Gil and I, and sometimes the little old ladies who wanted to fly out to see their grandchildren, seemed to be the passengers most often taken behind closed doors and told to bend over or squat. Then the authorities gave a free pass to the swarthy, bearded bastards with towels over their heads and maniacal glints in their eyes. Gil and I actually enjoyed driving to golf events as long as they weren't so far away that we felt like quadriplegics as we tried to exit the vehicle to eat, piss and stretch.

We loved taking the scenic routes, the back roads, sharing the driving to Houston, eating at the places the people in a hurry never get to enjoy, gazing at the countryside that so many other people never notice.

Taking the long, slow way also meant we got to say, 'You can have it' to the speed freaks zipping along I-45, in a hurry to get nowhere, jacked up on coffee, one hand on the wheel while yapping away on their cell phones, losing control of their GM pickups, ending up as crispy critters caught in masses of flaming, twisted steel. There are the lucky ones, too, the overturned eighteen-wheelers that dump their toxic sludge all over the highway and cause an all-day delay, and at the end of it the driver emerges from his cab, scratching his head, fresh from his nap.

I felt eager to play in the Houston Open this year because, for a nice surprise, they had decided to have it in the city itself, not some distant suburb. They were holding the Open at Cedar Lake, where I had played respectable golf and won some money.

The 16th at Cedar Lake demands that the golfer hit a big drive over a broad lake, and the green is shaped like a mountain, thus the poor guy has to hit his ball just so, or the ball will roll down the other side.

Gil Donaldo didn't like it. He swore he would never return. "Cedar Lake sucks," he told me.

"You're just mad because you finished twenty-ninth," I said.

"No, Grover, I'm fucking *thrilled* because I finished twenty-ninth."

On the drive back, we ate in one of the restaurants we'd stopped in on our way to Houston. We spoke of Lorna.

"How's it going with the Prick's momma? Thinking about making her Number Four? Don't mean to pry, just making conversation?" Gil asked.

I shrugged. "We haven't made any plans. Just being spontaneous and enjoying ourselves when we're together. I live in Bayporte and she lives in California, so our actual time together is pretty limited."

He nodded. "I've met couple like you. One's in Canada and the other is in the States, and they have to figure out, like which country they want to live in. You got to get married, then get a green card or whatever. It's application forms, interviews, fees, fingerprintings. What a fuckin' hassle."

"Well, she and I will worry about those hassles if and when they ever come up."

"I got a feeling," Gil told me, "that those hassles are gonna come up much faster than you think."

"Well, she sure doesn't act like she's in a hurry to get married. I mean, we've only been running around together for a few months."

"Maybe Number Four will be a charm," Gil said.

"I wouldn't call her Number Four, even if I did marry her."

"Seems to me that you married Helene, Alicia and Simone. Three wives, right? Three divorces?"

I shook my head. "Lorna wouldn't be Number Four. She would be Number One, the best lover I've ever had."

"Aw," said Gil, "that's awful sweet. 'Scuse me while I puke."

"Fuck you, Gil," I said, laughing.

"Grover, you need to be realistic. Women who are as beautiful as Lorna? Well, every man wants them, and they know it. No matter who you are, they'll get bored with you because all the other guys are hitting on her. They don't give a shit about that ring on her finger. Plus, she ain't wearin' no chastity belt. We don't live in Christian times when people say, 'I'm married and miserable, but I refuse to get a divorce because it's an un-Christian thing to do.' No, man, what they say is, 'I'll stay married till it's no fun, then I'll get a divorce.' Lorna's already gone through one divorce, so maybe she would divorce you, too."

"You don't have her figured right. She's an intelligent, mature woman, a mother and business professional. She has her shit together. She knows what she thinks. We have conversations."

"Do tell."

"We talk about music. She believes that the Beatles and Springsteen will still be popular in three hundred years. She got tired of Elvis and Michael Jackson years ago."

"Does she respect the Grateful Dead? She'd better."

"Are you kidding? She's from California—she *has* to

like the Dead. It's the law." I paused. "She doesn't like the Stones. She says they stopped being cool many years ago, and a rock band should retire once the young people out there start laughing at them."

"What are her politics?"

"She's against the death penalty. She thinks if you've done something totally heinous, they should lock you up for the rest of your life and force you to listen to Eminem and Niggers with Attitudes CDs."

"Cool."

"Yeah. You see what I mean, Gil? All your life, you've judged women by their looks. Lorna has smarts, too."

"Well, forgive me for being a guy," he said.

26

Back to the U.S. Open at Pinehurst. Sometimes, I'm luckier than I want to be. As I stood out there on day one and tried to reorient myself to the course, I got to meet Bruce Priklan.

Lance's father.

Lorna's ex.

I knew who he was right away, because he stood there next to Lance, who teed off one ball after another and drove it in the direction of Timbuktu. Bruce, a tall, tanned, buffed-out guy, had a full head of light hair that probably had been cut and colored for a few hundred dollars, and I thought he should have worn a T-shirt emblazoned with STILL A VAIN ASSHOLE AFTER ALL THESE YEARS.

Bruce had an iPhone pressed to his face and a burgundy golf shirt and khaki slacks covering his body. He also wore more gold rings, bracelets and neck chains than three crack dealers. I could tell by its glimmer that his bling was real, probably eighteen-karat. Certainly his Rolex was no Hong Kong knockoff. But why did he have that Louis Vuitton "man purse" slung over himself shoulder. And why was he wearing Air Jordans?

I walked up to them as Bruce pulled his iPhone away from his ear and put it into his man purse.

I said, "Hey, Lance, mind if I borrow your looks, talent and money for the day?"

Neither man laughed.

"Do you like Pinehurst, Grover?" Lance asked.

"I've done OK here," I replied.

"Yeah, but do you *like* it?"

"Do *you*?"

He shrugged. "It's no worse than some of the others."

"That's *my* answer, too," I retorted. To Bruce, I said, "How's it goin', eh?"

Bruce frowned. "Friend of yours, Lance?"

Lance said, "Dad, this is Grover Bobbitt. Grover, this here's my father."

"Oh, hey!" Bruce said, shaking my hand and giving it a sort of brotherly pump. I'd had him figured for the kind of guy who rips the Yellow Pages in half just to prove he can, and who breaks other guys' hands just to show he can do *that*, too.

"I should thank you," Bruce said.

"For what?" I asked.

"For making Laura so happy."

Laura?

"She's your ex, right?"

He nodded. "My biggest mistake."

I wasn't sure if he meant marrying her or divorcing her had been his "biggest mistake."

"If she and I ever reconcile"—he said with the utmost smugness, as if all things were possible when you were Bruce Priklan—"we'll remember our mistakes and try to learn from them. Right, Lancelot?"

Lancelot. I'll bet the kid loved that.

"Whatever you say, Dad." Lance swung and murdered another golf ball.

"I thought," I said to Bruce, "that you and Lorna were pretty much over and done with."

Bruce shrugged. "I still have deep feelings for her,

Grover, and my motto is, 'Never say never.'"

"Oh." Then, "I thought you'd remarried."

"I did, for a while. But she was too much like the women I've seen in porn videos. Outside of the bedroom, they just don't have much value."

"So you're a free man again?" I asked, not at all liking the sound of that and hardly eager to hear his answer.

Bruce laughed. "Yeah! That's a fine way of putting it! I assume Laura and you talk about these things, but maybe she hasn't given you a recent update. Want one?"

"An update? Yes, please."

"Well, I want Laura to come back to me."

"What?"

"To *work* for me. I have my own agency now, International Athletic Management. It's getting too big for me to control alone. This is happening mainly because my top client, who also happens to be my son, is making so much money. Also, I'm getting close to signing another client who will make me another huge pile of money. It's not a done deal, so I really can't say much about it. The client's name—are you ready?—is Hana Palmer. How's *that* for an acquisition?"

"She's fifteen," I reminded him. "She's too young for that. Anyway, her father is rich. She's set for life."

"Wrong. Mason Palmer is broke."

"How do you figure that?"

"Mason, in his very human eagerness to become the richest man in human history, recently made some very big, very bad financial decisions and now he is deeply in debt. His many assets are for sale and the banks are getting ready to send goons over to his house to shake him down."

"That's news to me," I said.

Bruce nodded. "It's a well-kept secret, so far. Even Hana thinks Daddy has their shit under control. That's why it's a secret: so that Mason's assets will retain their value long enough for him to unload it all and settle his debts. Grover, that guy own some cars you wouldn't believe. Vintage Bentleys, Rolls Royces, a few Lamborghinis..."

"And I guess they'll be yours soon."

He ignored this. "So I'm going to sign Hana and charge fifty percent instead of thirty because of her father's financial difficulties. Of course, I would give her a ten-million signing bonus, which would help her old man get his creditors off his ass."

"Will ten million help them that much?" I asked.

"It will give Mason some time to breathe and check his blood pressure. But mostly it will help me. I will then have Lance and Hana in my stable."

"Does Lorna know you're signing Hana?"

"Yes. I told her this morning."

I wanted to check my own blood pressure. I also wanted to kick Bruce's balls up through the roof of his mouth. But I kept listening as he kept talking.

"To be a player in the business side of things, I should move my main office to New York, which is where I seem to spend most of my time anyway. Then I would have Laura run my Beverly Hills office. I want her to sell the house in Pebble Beach, sell her interest in that art gallery to her partner and move permanently to Beverly Hills. She could get a perfectly good house not far from Rodeo and go shopping on her lunch."

"As what? Your manager?"

"No way. She would have equity in the firm. We're talking some serious coin she would be making,

Bobbs."

"So it would be just business, nothing personal?"

He shrugged.

Just then his iPhone rang. He answered it and handed it to me. "It's her. Talk."

"Lorna?"

"It's me. I know you're mad."

"Affirmative."

"I don't blame you, Grover."

"I'm so glad."

"We'll have a long talk later on," she said.

"We'll have plenty to say. I'm standing here with Bruce and Lance—"

"I know. I'm in the clubhouse, watching you. I didn't really want you to meet Bruce. He has a big fucking mouth. He says much more than he should."

"Affirmative. So, you're going to run his Beverly Hills office, eh?"

"Maybe. I'm not sure yet. There's a shitload of money involved in that matter. You need to help me make that decision."

"Why did you lie to me, Lorna?"

"I didn't lie. I just omitted a few things."

"As opposed to lying…"

"I'm sorry."

"I'm really pissed off," I told her. "And I have some golf to play today. I'm not in the best frame of mind to play."

"Do your best," she said.

I hung up.

"Think fast!" I flipped the iPhone back to Bruce. He caught it. "Nice seeing you boys, I think."

27

Anger, said Jock Kainer, my Oliver Johnson High School basketball coach, could be an athlete's best friend. He wanted us to go into each game being "hotter than July." Since we lived in Bayporte, where our Julys were often rainy and mild, I didn't altogether understand what he meant by that expression.

Kicking one's opponent in the scrotum could be a very effective tactic as long as the zebra didn't see you do it. Cracking the ribs of the other team's star player was a terrific way of putting him on the disabled list for the remainder of the season.

I took Coach Kainer's strategy seriously, especially on defense. "Make those bastards pay for every point they put on the scoreboard," he'd said.

Coach Kainer believed the best time for playing dirty was when the other guy was most vulnerable. "When he's got the ball in his hands and he's getting ready to shoot, that's when you hurt him because he can't defend himself. Punch him good and hard. Give him something he won't forget for a long, long time."

We played full-court defense and tried to psych out our opponents with trash talk about their mums, dads and siblings. If we knew this guy was best pals with that one, we would say, "How's your bum buddy over there?" If an opponent wore a crucifix on a chain, we might say the most sacrilegious filth right to his face, watch him go red, and snatch the ball from his hands.

I learned many life lessons from Coach Kainer, who always led us to city, provincial and national championships. He reminded us that humiliation and degradation were our best friends, if we had the balls to use such friends against our enemies. Our practice sessions were so long and difficult that our actual games, by comparison, seemed easy and fun.

Coach Kainer said, "It's not enough to be a stud on the playing field. You have to succeed in the classroom, too. Don't let me hear that any of you fell below a B average, or I'll bench you." The player who missed an easy basket in practice had to do fifty pushups in front of the squad. If he caught us in a fistfight, everyone had to run four hundred meters. Eventually, we all got shin splints.

What I will always remember about him was what he would say to us in the locker room before each game. No matter how many times he said it, his talk made my heart pound and gave me gooseflesh.

"Men," he would say, "tonight we are going to make Bayporte basketball or die trying. We are going to eat those guys for dinner and shit them out tomorrow morning!"

But, I wondered, how could I take that fire-in-the-belly rage and make it work for me out on the golf course?

I asked Everett about that as we stood at the tee for hole number one at the Open.

"So you mad at yo' girlfrien'," said Everett, "an' you want to git rid of that anger here on the golf course?"

"Yes."

"What ol' Jock tell you about girlfrien' problems in high school?"

"I'd be embarrassed to say."

Everett chuckled. "We both growed-up men. Ain't nothin' you can say that I ain't heard lotsa times before."

"He would say, 'Think of the cunt vomiting, picking her nose, taking a dump, chewing with her mouth open.'"

Everett laughed. "Lotsa guys be jerkin' off thinkin' about her doin' those things."

I laughed, too. But I realized I wanted to stay angry at Lorna, Bruce, International Athletic Management and every man who had won at least one major and had the love of a good woman.

I said to Everett, "Lorna's like, 'My ex is here but I didn't want to tell you. I wanted to protect you from something that might hurt you.' You want to know what really bugs me about all this? It's people who want to 'protect' me from something that might 'hurt' me. You know what I want to say to them? I want to say, 'I'm forty fuckin' years old, and I'm neither a child nor a retard, so don't 'protect' me, because I've already been through more 'hurting' than you'll ever know about."

"Well," Everett said, "you know the ol' sayin: 'Success is the best revenge.' So let's win this thing an' git some revenge on them folks thass been hurtin' po' Grover Bobbitt all these years."

28

For the first round, I played in a threesome with Stu Claudell and Thom Knutson, the latter being the man who wore tight slacks to show off his oversized, uncut *schlong*.

Both men had brought along their women. Cookie Claudell still needed at least ten thousand dollars' worth of dental work, and I wasn't turned on my chipped, discolored teeth, but Cookie's smile was so big, open and unembarrassed that I considered her pretty more than plain.

Soviette Knutson, Thom's fiancee, wore an outfit that screamed TRASHIEST WOMAN IN AMERICA. Her white shorts ran right up the crack of her butt and her zoomers threatened to burst out of her flimsy little halter. Her pink kinky boots showed off curvaceous legs, and her blonde hair hung even lower down her back than her husband's.

Soviette attracted more attention than we did. Her fans surrounded their slutty Russian rapper, ogling her jiggling mammaries and leering at their owner.

Perhaps Soviette's outfit was not entirely to blame for what happened. Her fans, clearly on a diet of retard sandwiches, had gotten a bit too friendly with their heroine.

I heard the shouting, screaming and yelling. Then I saw the pushing and shoving, even a tackle or two. Thom Knutson and I surveyed the crowd and went to see if we could be of help. Maybe he suspected his wife had something to do with the commotion. I know I did.

The golf carts arrived, too, and the officials emerged in their jackets and striped tie that made them look like boarding-school boys.

I recognized Sid James, the doofus currently running the USGA. He led his people into the fray and said to Soviette, "Madam, you are creating an unacceptable situation here at the Open."

Maybe he meant to grab her arm. Instead, he got hold of her right zoomer. She laid into him.

"Get your hand off my fucking titty!" she screamed, her English quite good. "I'll get you busted, you ugly fucking pervert! Who do you think you are? Who do you think *I* am? Tell me!"

Thom announced, "This lady…will be my wife as soon as my attorneys straighten things out. She is here as my personal guest. If you have any issues with her presence at this event, please speak to me."

Sid James said, "Mister Knutson, we have an issue with your fiancee's style of dress at this event. It is far beyond inappropriate."

"She is a professional performer," Thom said, "and sometimes her outfits are, well, flamboyant. But usually this is not a problem, as her many fans appreciate her unique sense of style. It is not our wish to make trouble. On the contrary, we wish to make peace. So, my beautiful girl, would it not be better for you to dress, well, more conservatively for this event?"

"*What?*" Soviette glowered at the man she would soon marry. "You take this asshole's side instead of mine? You think I am indecent, hey? Well, check me out!"

Soviette pulled up her halter and revealed her breasts. She spun, very slowly, three hundred sixty degrees to the sounds of whooping and wolf whistles and the blinding flashes of cell phone cameras.

Sid James and a few of his cronies grabbed and stuffed her into one of their golf carts. He said something to her I couldn't hear but his message could have been only one thing: *We are taking you back to the clubhouse. You will put on some clothes and mind your manners, or we will put you under house arrest.*

I heard Soviette scream at them, "Do you know who you're fucking with? I am a star! My husband is rich! We'll sue your asses off!"

Fay Dacell, the USGA's executive director, smiled and shrugged at Thom. "What can I tell you? They'll make her comfortable in the clubhouse, give her sandwiches and wine. She can chat with the other golf wives."

"Great zoomers," I told Thom.

I hit my tee ball and it went straight, if not that far. It landed in the middle of the fairway. As the spectators applauded and cheered, and I nodded my thanks, I felt once again that I really needed Lance Priklan's brute strength.

I hoped I would do that some more—hit the ball nice and straight, staying out of the rough.

So, after staying angry but not furious at Lorna Priklan, and having the good fortune of seeing Soviette Knutson show her mams—would the iPhone images of her be online yet? I sure hoped so, and would look into it as soon as I could—I spent all that day being mainly concerned with playing good golf.

Something curious happened, but not to me, and I felt relieved that it happened to someone else, yet I felt badly that it happened to Stu Claudell.

What happened was this: Stu hooked his tee ball and it ended up bouncing down a village road, out of bounds and out of sight. He teed up another one and drove it down the fairway, a couple of hundred yards from the green, whence he was shooting four.

But he hit this one wrong, too, and it went out of bounds.

"Shit turd motherfucker!" he yelled.

I feared his profane words could be heard throughout the Carolinas.

A few of us started looking through the area near the road. Cookie Claudell looked, too, nudging aside the pine needles and leaves as if they were clumps of feces and snarling at everything.

"Found it!" Stu called out. "Just a foot out of bounds!" As if that were something to be pleased about.

"You're now shooting six," I reminded him. "You'll be lucky to end up with eight."

"Too bad for me," he said.

By then we had all noticed the maroon Bentley that had been cruising towards us. It stopped, and the lady driving it said, to no one in particular, "Do you know where I can get a hotel room for the night?"

"How did you get past security?" I asked.

She shrugged. "I just did. It was easy."

Cookie said, "Just wait a bit. If my old man don't get

his shit together, we may be checking out *real* soon."

Later, in the press center, I congratulated Stu and Thom on playing well; they had tied at 74.

"It's easy to play well all day when you start off well," I said as the sports reporters tapped on their iPads and I spoke into their microphones. "What's difficult is getting off to a bad start and not getting so discouraged that you play badly throughout the day."

29

I looked up at the leaderboard, saw my name at the top and shuddered. I felt that way because I knew it wouldn't last very long, and people would say, "You were the leader of this thing, and yet you let it slip away. What's your problem?"

I had no problems, at least not at first. This course was a friend of mine, most of the time. I teed up my ball and drove it in the right direction. It stayed out of the pine forest, and my putts sometimes actually dropped right into the cup.

Everett liked it, too. He danced around the flag like Michael Jackson, pumping his hips and grabbing his junk. I said as much to him.

"Boss," he replied, "you keep playin' this good an' I'm gonna keep dancin'."

Stu had a quadruple bogey on the second hole and ended up four over par for that day. He'd lost his composure early on and seemed unable to recover. Thom also finished over par; that ugly incident involving his wife and her breasts left flustered and unsteady.

Thom went looking for Soviette at the 18th but couldn't locate her. He found Fay Dacer outside the clubhouse with a few enraged golf writers, telling the writers why they were no longer entitled to parking passes. He added that punching him out would be a very poor course of action on their part.

The writers walked away, admonishing Fay not to be terribly surprised if he discovered his own vehicle keyed up.

Fay said to Thom, "Soviette is in the clubhouse. She said she could drink a full bottle of Stolichnaya and it wouldn't impair her ability to function, but she was wrong. She's sleeping it off now."

The first question the reporters asked me was about Soviette's behavior earlier that day.

"It was nothing," I told them. "She's a celebrity, a performer. Her style is very aggressive and so are her fans. Today things got a bit crazy."

They asked if I knew her well.

"I got to know her a bit better today," I replied.

We all laughed.

They wanted to know if I liked her music.

"About as much as I like Eminem, Ice-T and Souleye," I said.

We all laughed some more.

"Here's something that will crack you up," I said, and told them about Stu's wayward ball, his glee in finding it, the lady in the fancy car and the clever thing Cookie said to her.

I omitted what happened as I walked off the 18th green. Cookie, the golf wife in need of dental work, came up to me, threw her arms around me and administered five minutes of tongue-fu. Before darting away to help her hubby find his ball, she gave me a smile and wink that said, *Next time you're out our way and my husband isn't around, we can do lots more of this—and more.*

Well, that kiss and smile were real, but the message may just have been wishful thinking. I have such thoughts, much too often.

. . .

The reporters knew how proud I was of my custom-made driver and asked if I felt it had helped my game.

They noted that throughout the day, I had hit my tee ball in the right direction and kept it in bounds.

I tried to be funny. Reporters always liked funny. It made their jobs easier. "Golf is always better," I told them, "when I play well and make lots of money."

I thought they would appreciate that. But then a fifteen-year-old cunt shot a 70 and came in second.

30

Lorna, the woman I thought of as my girlfriend, had been following me for most of the day. I could hear her cheers and occasionally saw her when I looked into the crowd. But mostly I pretended otherwise.

Lorna and I spoke for a little while just after Cookie had pried her tongue out of my mouth and bounded off.

Lorna marched up to me and said, "So?"

I shrugged

"Do you like women who have bad teeth?"

"I like women, period."

"Who was she?"

"You mean that woman who was comforting me?"

"Yeah. I 'm surprised she wasn't giving you a blow job."

"She said she'd pencil me in for later."

"I repeat: Who was she?"

"Stu Claudell's wife."

"Nice to see a happily married couple."

"They're a modern, open-minded couple," I said.

"Nice for them," she replied.

"Anyway, Laura," I said, "where's your husband?"

"My *ex*? He's flown back to New York. He had dinner with Lance last night and breakfast with me just before he left."

"And what," I asked her, "will be your job title at International Athletes Management?"

"I don't like your tone, Grover." Lorna folded her arms. "If you're going to cop an attitude with me, I'm going to walk away."

"So walk away. I have to go to the gift store and buy some T-shirts and caps for my friends back in Bayporte. It's a pain in the ass but I promised them I'd do it. If I don't do it now, I'll never get it done."

"Then I'll go with you and make sure the cashier doesn't try to tongue you, too."

The gift store, actually a huge transparent tent, stocked every kind of souvenir junk one could think of. They even had balls and clubs.

In a corner of the vast tent, we found Clark Irving sitting at a table, signing copies of his new book. Alas, nobody seemed to have any interest in him or his book.

"Sign the thing and they'll buy it," Clark told us as we stood before him. "An hour ago? Wow, you wouldn't believe how many we sold. I'm getting writer's cramp."

"Clark Irving of the Globe," I said, "this is Lorna Priklan, Lance's mother."

"Hey, how are ya?" Clark muttered as he continued signing books. A pretty woman meant very little to him unless she was a TV or radio host, a PR hotshot or someone else who could help sell his book.

"How'd you do today, Grover?" Clark asked.

I shrugged. "Sixty-seven."

"Not bad. But that ain't gonna win it," he said.

"You never know," I said.

"Yeah, you never know."

We walked away as he kept on signing books.

Lorna and I declared a truce. We agreed not even to touch each other until the conclusion of the U.S. Open. We had dinner with a few people—Jake Grimsley, Gil Donaldo and Lance Priklan. We spoke of little except golf, and Gil ordered a bottle of very expensive wine. He toasted me and my 67.

"To the man who made Pinehurst his bitch today," said Gil, holding his wineglass aloft.

"How clever and charming of you," retorted Lorna.

We all got together for dinner on Friday, too. All but one.

Lance Priklan shot a very disappointing 80. "That blew chunks," he said of it. "I missed the cut," he added. The upside was that he had time to engage in other sports.

"I'm going to the bar and see what's going on," he told his mum.

"Don't be an easy lay," she admonished him. "Don't let the little head do all the thinking. Don't put out for some skank who's already boffed everyone."

I felt good that day. I still had the lead by two strokes. I'd been my usual clumsy self that day but my putts dropped in. Stu and Thom also made the cut, probably because their women weren't around to nag the hell out of them.

Soviette stayed in her hotel room to work on a new "song." Thom said she had been inspired by the "Nazi" tactics the "pigs" had used against her after she flashed her breasts at us.

"She does her rap into her iPod," Thom said. "Her words are impossible to understand but her anger is straightforward. I don't know why she is so angry. I have given her quite a good life. Maybe that's the trouble."

I didn't know where Cookie had run off to, or with whom. I didn't ask. She would be back soon enough, and I would always pretend that our little moment together hadn't happened.

Jake Grimsley said, "Grover! You know that Gil and I made the cut?"

I nodded.

"You know," he continued, "that Tiger, Ernie and Rory missed it?"

"Hold me while I cry," I retorted.

"Everyone will be sorry to see that those three stars won't be here to pose for pictures, but I know you're the man to beat right now and you don't have to worry about those superstars anymore."

I shrugged. "Still plenty of quality talent out here."

Jake guffawed. "I love who you're paired with tomorrow."

I didn't love it. I was paired with Hana Palmer.

31

The day of round three started with a delicious breakfast and a less than tasty visit with Barney Smoltz, my badass agent, who had a business proposal for Gil Donaldo and me. He had flown down from New York and gotten a limousine from the nearest Carolina airport.

"You're overdressed," I said, pointing at his dark suit and paisley tie. "Who died? Not me, I hope."

"Funny guy. I'm here on business, so I dressed for it."

"Gonna make us a few million, hey?"

Barney didn't laugh. "Could be, Grover. Want to hear about it?"

"Talk."

"Ever hear of siliconcrete?"

"Can't say that I have."

"Ever heard of composites and alloys?"

I nodded. "Yeah, it's where you have one material and you mix it with another material to make a new, better material."

"That's the idea. There's this guy down in California. His name is Roderick Nowarre, and he's developed this material called siliconcrete. Roddy swears he'll be able to make the best golf clubs ever with it. Gives you a longer drive, durable as hell. All the tests prove it's terrific. You guys have the chance to get in on this before the rest of the world goes crazy over it. His thinking is, he wants Grover Bobbitt and Gil Donaldo in all media related to siliconcrete. You two will be the public faces of this exciting new product."

"Do you always call him 'Roddy'?" Gil asked.

"He likes it," Barney said. "Also, the marketing research indicates that the most significant growth segment in golf is gay males. Well, why not? They don't have any children to support and they take their fun and games very seriously. So he wants to call all the clubs he makes the Rod. You know how phallic-looking golf equipment is—clubs and balls. He wants to exploit all that."

Gil and I burst out laughing. Presently we were teary and red-faced, thumping on the table.

Gil made a mock-humorless face and said in an effeminate pitchman's voice, "Hi, guys, I'm Gil Donaldo with the Rod. Well, actually I have two rods but the one I'm going to show you is the golf club right here"—he began stroking an imaginary club as if he were masturbating—"and in a moment Grover Bobbitt will show you *his*, which is just as long and stiff as mine…"

Barney rolled his eyes and turned to me. "I guess you don't want in on this either?"

"You're an astute man, Barney Smoltz."

"If you can deal with selling golf clubs to homos," Barney said, "this could become a *very* lucrative enterprise."

"We can't deal with homos," I said. "What else you got for a couple of straight guys who want to make a few bucks on the side?"

Barney tapped on his iPad a few times, then made us a few other offers.

"Don, you could do a golf clinic for a bunch of executives in Mexico."

Don shook his head. "No habla Espanol."

"Don't matter," Barney said.

"Matters plenty," Gil said. "How else am I gonna say, 'Sorry, amigo, but I can't marry your sister and get her a green card.'"

"For you, Grover," Barney said, "I can get you five thousand dollars to play in a tournament in Germany. "

"I'd rather sell golf clubs to queers."

Barney and his Rod-talk kept me giggling as I practiced that day. Lorna smiled and waved from the gallery. Tiger, Phil and the other studs who'd missed the cut gassed up their Gulfstreams and flew off. Still, many fans had remained to see how this tournament would end.

I wondered how many of those spectators were thinking, *After all this expense and hassle, I don't even get to see Tiger or the other superstars. Still, they let that tall, pretty girl play in this one, so maybe she'll be worth watching. But who's the dork she's playing with?*

The tall 15-year-old cutie walked up to me with her hand outstretched. "Hello, Mr. Bobbitt, I'm Hana Palmer."

I shook it. "Hi, Hana. Call me Grover."

She smiled and nodded. Almost my height. Up close, without makeup, her face had the dewy freshness of being new. Hana's dark-blue eyes were big and innocent, her smile wide and warm. She had the sweet insouciance of someone to whom nothing terrible had ever happened.

"Break a leg," I told her.

"Right back at you." She smiled as she walked back

to the tee.

I looked over to the fans behind the rope and saw Hana's father, Mason, standing on one side of the rope and her caddy on the other side, inches away. Mason seemed to be giving the caddy last-minute advice or threats. The daddy scowled, glowered and poked his finger at the caddy.

The caddy nodded and looked down as Mason probably assured him that if Hana didn't win the Open, Mason would hold the caddy personally responsible for the young lady's disappointing performance.

Everett said, "You think that girl can keep her poise with a daddy like that?"

"Daddy's full of shit and she knows it. If he gets out of line, she'll kick his ass."

I laughed. "How would a guy get her panties moist?"

"A Tesla Roadster and an American Express black card would be a good start."

Our first hole was a straightforward 400 yards with very little in the way of roughs or bunkers. Nice and clean, just hit it hard.

I didn't want the world to see a teenaged girl hit a ball longer than I did, so I used my best driver and whacked my tee ball as hard as I could. It made a nice arc and settled relatively close to the green.

"OK, go-go girlie," I muttered, "try beating *that*."

But then she stepped up to the tee, made her usual beautiful swing and did exactly that.

32

On the 8th hole, the go-go girlie lost her greatness. I felt sorry for the poor kid. I really did.

Pinehurst's 8th hole is very long and curves to the right. Hana's problem started when her tee shot ended up far to the left and in an uneven section of the fairway. She swore and snarled.

I wanted to say, "Don't overreact. You're not in such bad shape. If you're as good as they say, you'll make par for this hole."

Hana tried a chip shot, as she should have done, but didn't hit it hard enough and it rolled right back down to her. She did it again, and again. She looked skyward, her lips moving, and I felt glad that I couldn't hear what she said or thought.

Hana finally got to the green and nailed a thirty-foot putt that consoled her not at all.

Triple-bogey 7. Now she trailed me by—what? Five strokes?

We walked along together, she red-faced and sweating, lips pursed, hands clenched.

"Stay positive," I told her. "Just keep breathing and cool out."

She said nothing. She just looked down and away, in the opposite direction of her father.

"Back there," I continued, "when your ball came rolling back to you? You looked like you were about to hit it again while it was still moving. If you had actually done that, you would have been severely penalized—"

"Don't tell me the rules," she said. "I know them as

well as you do."

"Excuse me?"

"Which part of 'I know the rules' didn't you understand?"

"Maybe you do know the rules."

"Oh, I know the fuckin' rules, *Grover.*"

"OK, Hana, you know the rules. You don't have to use that kind of language. It's unprofessional and impolite."

"Fuck, fucker, fuckface."

Suddenly she didn't seem like such a sweet-faced cutie any more. Now she seemed like a spoiled brat who was copping a shit attitude because things weren't going her way. She'd spent her young life watching everything fall into place just fine, and when any problem ever came up, Daddy made it go away.

I spaced out for a few minutes and started thinking about teenagers. When Gil and I were growing up, our parents insisted that we call adults "sir" or "ma'am," and that, especially in restaurants, we resist the urge to play with our food or chew with our mouths open. Today's teenagers, males in particular, get tattoos and piercings all over, listen to music with insipid lyrics and, for conversation, repeats the nonsense he hears on MTV. Gil Donaldo liked to say he would like to take every upper-class, snot-nosed white boy who wore his baseball cap sideways and his jeans down around his ass-crack and make him spend six months in a real ghetto, then let him out and ask him how it felt to be "a bro in the 'hood."

Hana and I stayed silent for the next couple of hours. We really got down to the business of playing golf and sinking putts, which we mostly did.

I looked at the party ahead of us and tried really,

really hard to follow the keep-cool advice I had given Hana.

Ferret Chalmers made all of his putts, too, and some of them were far more difficult than mine. The scoreboard said he was about one stroke behind me.

Ferris "Ferret" Chalmers, arguably the least popular golfer I had ever met, loved being a douche bag and worked hard at it. Half a dozen years earlier, after winning every amateur competition worth playing in, he had turned pro. He promptly won two majors and many others, and alienated everyone by firing his caddy, who was also his daddy. Ferret accused his father of stealing money from him, then fired practically everyone who worked for him, rehiring some and then firing them again. His agent had taken 30 percent of Ferret's winnings, so now the golfer represented himself. He had even said goodbye to his bevy of girlfriends, who wore his name tattooed on their thighs and shoulders.

Tough shit for Ferret, I said to myself. But soon I forgot all about him, because something happened that brought despair to everyone in the Grover Bobbit fan club.

33

On the 18th hole, I couldn't decide which club to use, and indecision, particularly for a golfer, is necessarily a bad thing. So I went with my usual driver.

That hole, par-4 and several football fields long, doglegged right and had plenty of uneven parts, with trees to the right and a practice range to the left. I needed to hit my tee ball nice and hard to get it onto the green, because if it landed in the middle of the fairway, I would probably need to take three or four whacks to get it onto the green.

I reared back and swung my club with much anger but little direction. I groan as I watched my ball go into the forest.

"Don't feel too bad," Everett said. "You hit it hard, so maybe it cleared the trees."

"Maybe it didn't."

I said to Hana, "I'm going to tee up again, in case my other ball isn't playable."

I did just that, and hit the ball with the utmost care. It ended up on the fairway, pretty much where the first one should have gone.

"I'm gonna go have a look for that first one," I said, and soon I was waving at Everett and smiling. My ball was still very playable, and I wouldn't triple-bogey that hole after all.

"Grover," said Hana Palmer as Everett and I stood talking, "I'm going to call a ruling on you."

"You're gonna *what*?"

"I demand that you play your second ball."

And *I* demand that you shut your yap, silly child, before I take you over my lap and tan your ass.

"I have no idea what you're talking about."

"You violated the rules," she said.

"I did? When?"

"Just now. You committed a verbal."

"I did not. You were the one dropping F-bombs earlier. I didn't try to penalize you for that."

"I don't mean profanity. Before you hit your second tee shot, you failed to tell me that you were shooting a provisional ball."

"I certainly did."

"You certainly didn't."

"Damn right I did."

"Do you remember what you said *verbatim?*" she asked.

"Yeah. I said, 'I'm gonna tee up again, in case my other ball isn't playable.'"

She nodded. "You failed to use the word 'provisional.' The rule book says that a player must say, 'I'm going to play a *provisional* ball.' That is a violation. I am invoking the penalty. You must play the second ball."

"Not too freakin' likely. I want to hear from a rules official."

"Speaking," came a voice from behind me.

I turned around and saw a slim, gray-haired woman wearing a blue jacket, khaki slacks and a USGA armband. I might have thought her pretty except for the grim set of her mouth.

"I'm Holly Brendan, a vice-president of the USGA. As Hana says, you must play the second ball."

I took a deep breath and said, "Do you have any clue how much is at stake here? I'm gonna need a second opinion on this. Your ruling could cost me my lead, and I'd never get it back."

Holly Brendan nodded and spoke into her radio. "Valentine? Are you there? It's Holly."

I asked myself, Is there really someone out there named Valentine?

"We have a situation on eighteen. Need you here."

"Who's coming?" I asked.

"Valentine Gersbach," said Holly, lifting her chin.

"Never heard of her."

"Valentine is a man," said Holly, narrowing her eyes. "He's won some seniors' titles of much significance."

"That right, eh?" I retorted in my goofiest Canadian accent.

Holly Brendan wheeled around and walked away. She pulled out her iPhone and yakked away as she gazed at the trees.

I stood there, wishing for the first time in a long while that I hadn't given up cigarettes years earlier. I would have settled for a candy bar—just something to put into my mouth and concentrate on.

Valentine Gersbach rolled up in a cart to where Holly Brendan stood by the trees. Holly talked and gesticulated; Valentine listened and nodded. The two came to me, he driving and she walking.

"I uphold her decision," said Valentine.

"You're full of crap," I said. "I want a real official, the chairman of the competition committee. Get his ass up here."

"He may be unavailable at the moment," Valentine told me. "I saw him having lunch in one of the hospitality tents."

"What's his name?"

"James Morrison Weatherby Dupree."

I groaned. "He's the guy who diddled me over at the Masters."

"Mister Bobbitt! Such language!"

"Get Dupree up here," I told them.

Valentine Gersbach nodded and got Dupree on his radio. They spoke for several minutes, then Gersbach handed his radio to Holly Brendan, who spent at least ten minutes with Dupree. Finally she returned the radio to Dupree.

Within ten minutes, we saw Dupree riding a cart towards us.

"Mister Bobbitt," he said, shaking his head, "you are becoming someone I'm having to deal with. While I was having lunch in the tent, I spoke to Valentine and Holly. They told me what was happening and I made my ruling over the radio. All I'm going to do now is tell you what I told them."

"Yes...?"

"Their ruling stands. It's in the book. You have to play ball number two."

"Shit."

"You see, it's a rule that your competitors have the option of ignoring or invoking. Miss Palmer chose to invoke it, so I'm obligated to enforce her invocation. Now, I've got to get back and finish my lunch." Dupree sped off.

"Everett," I said, "we just lost this thing."

"It ain't a done deal jest yet."

"It sure as fuck is."

Valentine Gersbach said, "Mister Bobbitt, you need to hurry up and finish this hole. I'm giving you a time limit."

I hooted. "What for? How come we need a time limit? Is there anyone behind us? No. I don't fucking think there is."

"Please! Mister Bobbitt! That's unsportsmanlike conduct!"

"So is this." I turned around, dropped my pants and showed him my big, white, pimply Canadian ass. Then I hit my ball here and there until, a dozen putts later, I finished up. Probably in last place.

34

"I will go down in golf history for all the wrong reasons," I told Lorna over dinner. "Golf loves these instances where some guy is leading the pack and has a shot at winning a major—and then his whole game falls apart. People will look at my stats and say, 'Bobbitt was playing good golf and could have won that Open. But *ten* putts on the last hole! Did the poor bastard have a meltdown out there?'"

We sat in the hotel's dining room. Only a few people remained; the Open had ended and just about everyone who had arrived for it was now gone. I had finished third; Ferret Chalmers had won, and Hana Palmer placed second.

I had promised myself to cut back on booze, but weakened when the server took our drink orders. I drained my third Canadian Comfort over ice and sighed.

Lorna swallowed a mouthful of shrimp and said, "Your purse for this thing was a nice payday. Doesn't that make you smile?"

"I wanted that trophy. I always want the trophy. I've had my share of 'nice paydays.' The trophy is the thing." I took another sip of Canadian Comfort. "You notice what a good sport I was at the ceremony? I smiled so hard my teeth hurt. I resisted the urge to say, "Gee, Ferret, now I guess you'll be an even more insufferable bastard.' He congratulated me for being resilient enough to overcome my 'bad break' like I was Joe Theismann after Lawrence Taylor fell on him."

Lorna shuddered. "Oh, don't bring that up. I remember that on Monday Night Football. I could hear the *crack!* when his leg broke. The announcers heard it, too. They sounded like they wanted to cry or puke."

"After the Open, my mum and dad phoned to say winning isn't everything and I'm doing something I love, which is more than what most people get in life."

"How kind of them."

"Ferret said that my good play inspired him to play better. In the locker room, the other guys shook my hand and congratulated me, or maybe they were consoling me for puking up the lead."

"They were congratulating you."

"Gil Donaldo said, 'Grover, you came so damn close this time, you just need to keep the faith. And I'm an atheist!'"

Lorna nodded. "Keep the faith. Good advice."

Jake Grimsley said, "We were all cheering for you. We didn't want Ferret or Hana to get it."

"My sentiments exactly," said Lorna.

"Barney Smoltz said, 'Them the breaks, kid. But maybe this heartbreaker can turn out to be a good thing for you. More endorsements."

"Nice. Anyone else?"

"Yeah. Thom Knutson said, 'Soviette and I really feel for you, especially her. She says she's going to write and record a song about the importance of not letting the bastards grin you down.'"

Lorna said, "I'm sure it'll be a major hit."

"Simone Allerd—"

"Your ex—"

"And business partner and close friend. She tweeted me, 'So your English teacher at Oliver Johnson was a cunt. Life goes on.' Made me laugh in spite of myself."

So we sat there, and I forced myself to eat the steak I had ordered. My Canadian Comforts over ice, instead of stimulating my appetite, had made me drunk and morose. Lorna said, "I don't want to sound like a bitch, Grover, but when you lost patience with yourself and Dupree and started putting the ball all over the green…well, that was immature and unprofessional."

She sounded like a bitch. "I should have punched out Dupree, then kicked Hana's ass. Do you think I could take her in a fight? She's tall and strong, but as long as she didn't slam her foot into my nut-sack—"

"Grover, grow up."

"What? We're just having dinner and I'm telling you what's on my mind."

"I like that tweet Simone sent you. She sounds like my kind of gal. I'd like to meet her."

I sighed. "Yeah, she thinks every life experience is an opportunity for growth. This Open disappointment is supposed to make me a larger, freer, more loving person. God makes me lose tournaments because He loves me so much. I wish He would start loving somebody else."

"I guess you're God's special son. You should feel very blessed."

"Well, I don't." Then, "How about Hana Palmer? I don't know if she's God's special daughter, but He's sure given her more golf talent than any kid her age has a right to have."

"She's said she feels really badly about that rule she invoked."

"When did she say that?"

"In the press tent. I read it on my iPad," Lorna said. "She said she made such an issue of your playing a provisional ball just because she wanted to shake you up."

"For real? She said 'shake me up'?"

"Yes. You took the lead, and she started falling behind, so she tried to mess with your mind by making trouble for you with the officials. The thing was, she didn't think her invocation would be upheld. She wanted you to get mad and lose your poise so you would bogey the hole."

"You read that on your iPad?" I asked, disgusted.

Lorna nodded. "Hana said they taught her that at the clinic in Florida. They spent hours and days instructing her in subtle and more overt ways of psychologically injuring her opponent during competition."

"Is that what they taught her? No coach or mentor ever taught *me* any dirty tricks. I had to learn them on my own."

She smiled. "Funny guy. Anyway, I'm just telling you what I've read. In your case, the bad guys were the officials who ruled against you."

"Sticking up for Hana now, eh?"

"Don't be nasty."

"Who's being nasty? She's going to become one of your clients, right? When you join International Athletes Management. Bruce said so himself. He has this verbal agreement with Hana about representing her."

"I am *not* a part of IAM. Not yet, anyway, and maybe never. He's made me an offer. I'll have to think about it. Understand?"

"I don't care for your tone of voice," I said. "Am I not allowed to be angry because of what's just happened to me?"

"Look, Grover—"

"You know what, Lorna?"

"Tell me."

"How long have we been a couple? A few months? For most of that time, I've been thinking that I'm in love with you. It's been wonderful, and it's something I didn't think would happen to me. I've been divorced by three women who found me totally unacceptable as a husband, and I've been walking around thinking that, as a husband or boyfriend, I'm nobody's bargain. So I meet you, and you're sexy as hell, and you seem to care about me every bit as much as I care about you. Who woulda thunk that I, a forty-year-old, three-time loser at love, would get seriously involved with someone like you? But something else is going on, too. While all this lovey-dovey thing is happening, I lose two majors that I should have won. Not just one, but two. Frankly, Lorna, I'm the most superstitious golfer alive, and I'm starting to think you have totally jinxed my golf game."

Fuck you and your golf game, Grover, Lorna mouthed before she got up and left the dining room.

PART THREE

36

I had to admit that, throughout my life, I had quite a talent for saying the wrong thing, even though I believed I was saying the true and honest thing. At dinner, Lorna got mad and stayed that way for quite a while. I needed to reclaim my love life before the start of the British Open.

Lorna checked out of her hotel the next morning after my overdose of Canadian Comfort had accused her of costing me a couple of majors. I knew how angry I'd made her when the desk clerk told me Lorna hadn't left me a note.

I flew back to Bayporte, hung out at home until my hangover had mostly gone, then tried to figure out how to get back with Lorna. I knew she would be at her home or art gallery. Or maybe she'd gone to see her ex, Bruce, about accepting his offer to work at International Athletes Management. If so, she would be in Beverly Hills or New York.

Oddly, when I called the agency's offices, they said, "Lorna Priklan? Bruce's ex? Never heard of him. Didn't know he'd ever been married. Sorry."

Katie Sanford, Lorna's business partner, told me that my heartbroken lover had come home but had no desire to see me ever again.

"She's thinks I'm some kind of asshole, eh?" I asked.

"Oh, sure. Worse than that. Something that requires your personal presence."

"Is she there? Mind if I speak to her?"

"She won't take your call."

"Tell her for me—"

"Get down here and tell her yourself."

"She knows freakin' well how much I value her."

"Does she?"

"I should start reading those women's magazines so I would know how to handle these matters," I said.

"Funny guy."

"Maybe I should serenade her. Hold the phone away from your ear, in her direction. I'll sing as loud as I can."

"Cracking wise won't win her back, Grover."

"I'm just really frustrated, Katie. I'm trying to fix this thing, but how can I do that when she won't even speak to me?"

"Tell you what, Grover. Fly down here, get the best suite in Pebble Beach, order in flowers and champagne and invite her over. Ideally, your seduction will be successful."

"Not a bad suggestion, Katie, but Lorna is so mad at me that the seduction would probably fail."

"Well, if she says no, I'll let you get *me* drunk and laid."

"Funny girl."

While in Bayporte, I stopped by Afternoon Delights, Simone Allerd's chocolate hangout, to make sure that my bills were being paid on time. I feared that my secretary-for-the-time-being had been partying too hard to worry about keeping my creditors quiet.

Ever since I had been on the road well over half the

year, I'd hired someone in Bayporte to be my secretary for the mundane stuff. For the big, important matters like investments, taxes and retirement funds, I had Barney Smoltz and his crackerjack staff in New York.

Barney's people had taken good care of me; at least, none of them had run off to the Bahamas yet with my money.

Alas, some of my Canadian bookkeepers had concluded that what was mine was also theirs, and by the time I wizened up to their shakedowns, they'd sped off in their new Mercedes and Beemers.

My current helper had been with me for a couple of years. A graduate in something from Northup, she managed Afternoon Delights' catering office and agreed to become my overpaid secretary. Her name was Barb or Brenda; I didn't see her often enough to remember. Maybe if she'd had a prettier face or better zoomers…

She also answered my emails and did much Facebooking and tweeting for me. I was naturally a smartass who had plenty of trouble conferring helpful advice, so as my public face, she helped make the world believe that I was a nice guy, or at least not a total dick.

She didn't read emails that were clearly from my exes. One came from Alicia Theodore, the ex who had spent most of her adult life helping a sleazy lawyer gain acquittals for riff raff.

Alicia's boss, Tad, didn't pay her especially well, but I did. She hit me up for non-repayable "loans" that she insisted were for a car repair or kitchen appliance. Most of the time, I knew, she used my money to go crazy at Neiman Marcus online or give to her latest live-in lover, some well-hung goof who wanted to drink beer and roll joints all day.

She'd recently emailed me a request for $30,000. "Simone would love to hear about it."

"She's busy in the kitchen," said Barb or Brenda. "We're doing the desserts for the gala of a bunch of Bayporte millionaires with a generous streak."

"Fundraising, eh? Who gets the money? The Diabetes Association?"

She laughed. Presently we got Alicia out of the kitchen. She wore chef's whites, stained with much chocolate, and faded old jeans. Still, she was one of the prettiest women I had ever known. We sat in her office and she poured herself a huge mug of coffee.

"Alicia sent me this." I handed her my iPhone. I had saved the message on the device. Simone read it aloud.

"'Dear Grover: I know I am always after you for some kind of practical help, but this time it is really an emergency. I have nobody else to ask because all of my family members have died from this or that.

"'Now my problem is that my health insurance will not cover the cosmetic surgery I need.'" In Canada, everybody must carry government-issued health insurance.

"'None of us is getting any younger, Grover, and I feel the need to get this medical treatment. Mainly what I need is a rhinoplasty, and a breast augmentation wouldn't hurt, either.'"

Simone laughed. "So now she wants a nose job and a boob job. I guess she thinks you're made of money."

"She *wants* the surgery. She doesn't *need* it. You've met her. She's a cutie." Then, "Anyway, I have a bigger problem right now."

Simone nodded. "Talk to me."

She already knew that I had taken up with a woman named Lorna Priklan. A month or so earlier, when I had popped into town for a few days, Simone and I went to lunch. I told her that Lorna was the loveliest woman I had ever met who wasn't named Simone and that I truly believed I could be happy with Lorna for the rest of my life. Then I told Simone about Pinehurst and dinner and that you're-a-jinx remark.

What, I wanted to know, could I do to get her back?

Simone and I had gotten married a couple of decades earlier because we enjoyed banging each other silly. We divorced the following year because of our poverty.

Back then, I was still trying to make money as a golfer. I didn't know, or care, about much of anything except swinging clubs, playing cards, going to movies, hanging out and sleeping in. She suggested that we split up, and I agreed. I let her go because I believed I didn't deserve her in the first place. We stayed friends and kept banging away when we got horny enough. Then I started remarrying and Simone just became a good friend.

She hadn't laughed at me for putting rings on Helene and Alicia, and she was always nice when meeting the strippers and other party girls who kept me company during my divorces.

Simone had remained a most alluring woman and I kept wondering why she remained single. She had acknowledged to being in one or two "fulfilling relationships," whatever that meant. Lately, however, she had been dateless, and happily so—she wanted to spend as much time as possible with her "top priorities," specifically Afternoon Delights and Hank and Charlie, her two poodles.

"As for Lorna," she was saying, "it's too bad you aren't Kobe Bryant or Sidney Crosby. You could go to

Boccasio's and buy her a million-dollar ring as a way of saying, 'I'm so sorry. Can you ever forgive me?' Women tend to respond very well to such gestures."

"Doesn't surprise me."

"I've got another idea."

"Hope it doesn't mean a trip to Boccasio's."

"Try dating some ugly women."

I shook my head. "One, I find female ugliness repulsive. Two, ugly women have an attitude because they know they're ugly and they hate themselves."

"Go out with someone who's disabled."

"Would *you* date a disabled person?"

She smirked. "It depends on which part of him was disabled."

"His love muscle."

She laughed and stood dup. "Grover, I have to get back to work. I think you already know what you need to do: Fly down to California and confront Lorna. Tell her how much you love her and that if she doesn't take you back, you'll be heartbroken for the rest of your life. She'll take you back because she loves you just as much as you love her. I know about these things."

She gave me a long, moist goodbye kiss as I squeezed her zoomers. Then I left.

37

I made sure I got a table at Club XIX at the Lodge in Pebble Beach because I knew the owners were going to close the restaurant soon. I also knew that if Lorna could be sweet-talked by me in that place and still tell me to go fuck myself, nothing would work and I'd simply have to find myself a new woman.

Lorna entered the crowded restaurant and three dozen heads turned as I pulled out a chair and she sat across from me.

"The only reason I'm here," she told me, "is that Katie said she'd go in my place if I stood you up."

"She was teasing you," I replied.

"Not at all. You're single and so is she."

Lorna ordered a Stolichnaya over ice, and I asked for another Canadian Comfort.

"Always Canadian Comfort?" she wanted to know.

I shrugged. "Sometimes a martini, but they get me drunk too fast. Canadian Comfort lets me stay in control a bit longer."

"So, here we are. Start begging my forgiveness."

I said that I was deeply in love with her, which was cliched as an old movie but absolutely true. I told her I had been miserable that awful evening when I made that retarded remark about her being a jinx. Right now, I said, I wanted to keep loving her and marry her and spend the rest of my life with her, because I knew she was the finest woman I had ever met.

"You haven't made a single joke yet," she said.

"No jokes tonight. You're seeing the serious,

humble Grover."

"He's boring. I like the jokes better."

"The jokes will be there when you want them."

"Have you rented a room here?"

I nodded.

"With a nice big bed?"

I smiled.

I wanted Lorna to see my suite so she could strip us both naked and ride my dick all evening. But when we got up there, she said, "I'm dying for a cigarette."

The state of California had decided that smoking was worse than child pornography. The anti-smoking lobbies had gotten tobacco consumption banned throughout the state. Gil Donaldo said, "It's OK for the fairies in San Francisco to blow each other in glory holes, but smoking in public? Bad stuff, man."

Lorna knew she shouldn't smoke in my suite. The wetbacks on the housecleaning staff, if they smelled her secondhand smoke, would report it to management, but fuck 'em.

"You just light up, sweetie," I told her as I looked through the minibar for more intoxicants.

"Thanks. I'll do that." She used a coaster for an ashtray and fired up a Newport as she plopped onto a sofa.

"I thought you might be getting naked."

"Why?"

"Sexual intercourse."

She blew out a long stream of smoke. "We have things to talk about."

"Yeah. I want you to go overseas with me."

Her moth dropped open. "We haven't even made up and now you want to travel with me?"

"We're making up right now. We can keep making up on the plane trip to Scotland."

"That one speech you made? That bit of sweet-talk and all is just fine and dandy?"

I shrugged.

"We have *issues*, Grover."

"Do we? I love you and you love me. The rest is simple and easy enough. We decide if we want to live in Canada or the States."

"There's more to it than that."

"Is there?"

"Yes," she said. "There's much more."

"Only if you want to complicate it."

"We have differences to reconcile."

I frowned. "We have differences? Sure. But who the fuck needs to reconcile them? I'm a man and you're a woman. That's a huge difference between us, but we still manage to have a very viable and symbiotic relationship."

"We disagree on so many things, Grover. Do you honestly think we can make it work anyway?"

"Shit, I *know* we can. My mum and dad have never agreed on anything for any period of time, and good for them. It gave them something to yell and scream about. It kept them interested in each other."

"Why did I come here?" Lorna rolled her eyes and stubbed out her cigarette. "Are we stuck in *American Graffiti*? Is this Nineteen Sixty-two? Are we going from the makeout point to an ice cream parlor to get a banana split?"

"Sounds good to me."

"Don't be flippant. I need to know where you're going in life so that I'll know where *we're* going."

"For the time being," I told her, "I am going to keep playing golf."

"But what about later on? In five, ten, fifteen years?"

"Lorna, I have a few good years of golf left in me."

"That's not the message you've been sending me. In the time we've known each other, you've been bitching about your age and how much you've deteriorated. So, what will you do? Become a golf instructor? Become some sort of entrepreneur?"

I shrugged. "Haven't thought about it much. Just living life one day at a time."

Lorna glowered at me through a pall of cigarette smoke.

I snapped my fingers. "Got it! When I can't make the Tour any longer, I'll shack up with one of those rich old widows. I'll wear pink blazers and ravish her every night."

Lorna rolled her eyes.

"I spoke to Bruce yesterday. We had a long phone call. Said some things, worked out some stuff."

"He's a handsome man. Does he have a big cock?"

"Would you rather hear about his cock or his business proposal?"

"Oh, his cock."

"Grover, I have a feeling that Bruce is going to become one of the top sports agents in the world," Lorna said. "As long as I've known him, he's had that eye of the tiger. He goes after what he wants and gets it. Now his thing is his sports agency. He has Lance and will soon have Hana. Bruce is an astute money manager, an eloquent salesman and a shameless, persuasive liar. He's fairly smart and *very* savvy."

"Sounds like a sports agent or a politician," I said.

"Well, he would be an outstanding sports agent, considering all of his personal qualities. His big weakness is infidelity. He is much too generous with his cock, especially when the girl is barely old enough to drive a car."

"Tell me about the offer."

"I would own a third of the company and earn half a million to start."

"Is that a good offer?"

"Well, it ain't fuckin' bad. Bruce has known me forever. He trusts me implicitly. He knows he can leave me alone to do my job and I won't screw it up. He wants to draw up a contract with the details spelled out. He would continue to run the New York office and do the stuff he likes—talking the talk, shaking the hands, travel to wherever the most promising young jocks are and get them to sign with him before any other agent does. I would do all the boring, behind-the-scenes stuff. I told him I wouldn't consider working in the Beverly Hills office because I just don't like that place."

"So you would move the office. To where?"

"I told Bruce that since I was in love with this Canadian guy in Bayporte, that would be the obvious choice."

"How did he feel about that?"

"Oh, he didn't mind. Bayporte is such a big city. Travel would work OK, and American businesses expand into Canada all the time."

"So are you going to sign that contract?"

"Don't know yet. There may be something in it for you. Think about when you will no longer be able to play golf well enough to make a living at it. How about taking an *executive* position at International Athletes

Management?"

I guffawed.

"Hello?" She lit up another Newport.

"Do you mean 'executive' or 'flunky'?"

"Grover, don't piss me off."

"I'm not *trying* to piss you off."

"Did I say 'flunky'? No, I don't think so. I said 'executive.' And you wouldn't have to retire from golf this Friday and begin your *executive* position on Monday morning. You can still play golf until you feel it's time to call it a career, whenever that may be, and that *executive* position will still be there, waiting for you. Also, you and I would be working together, as a team. You are an athlete, you know golf, you know people in other sports. You would be a huge asset to the agency, so don't think this is some kind of charitable gesture on the agency's part."

I went over to her. She stood up, and I put my hands around her waist.

"I guess what you're saying," I told her, "is that I better think long and hard about this matter, because if I say no, we're history."

"Not at all. I'm probably going to take this job, and if you come on board, too, we'll just have to work together and live together and learn to put up with each other."

"And what happens if I say that I would be perfectly willing to go along with it?"

"I would say, 'Let's get naked for sexual intercourse.'"

38

Puny hotels in towns where the British Open is played are usually the kinds of dumps that Edgar Allan Poe used to write about. Jones House, my small hotel in Carnoustie, sat in the middle of town, next door to Scots Arms, a bed-and-breakfast.

Everett, my caddy, was staying at the Scots Arms with my golf clubs. He had flown in the week before and spent a few nights in London, shopping, sightseeing and shagging English whores. He had paid several hundred dollars for trains and taxis from London to Edinburgh to Carnoustie.

Some of the more envious caddies said that Everett had a higher standard of living than I did.

I suppose I could have stayed at the Carnoustie Resort, a big new resort a few minutes from the golf course. But Tiger, Rory and a bunch of other studs had helped themselves to most of the rooms, and I got what they had left—a fancy, fresh-smelling jail cell.

Lorna was flying in on the weekend, and I knew she would be happier in Jones House, with a fireplace, sitting room, kitchenette and washroom. Her own private washroom? In Scotland, that is a rare treat indeed.

I also decided to hire a driver instead of killing myself and others by trying to tool along on the wrong side of the road.

My driver, James, met me at the airport and gave me a quiet drive out to Carnoustie. I thought of how many times I had gotten off this plane or driven into that city, quite ignorant of where the fuck to go or what to do. I guess I liked that feeling of being lost in the world. Grover, the eternal tourist.

I had arrived a week early to practice, but also because I felt better than I had in a long time and wanted to get oriented to my new course so that I would have every conceivable advantage.

I had never actually played in Carnoustie. I'd heard stories, of course, about challenging it could be. Coldest, clammiest, windiest, most unforgiving son of a bitch this side of the Atlantic. So I got there before the others did and practiced plenty. I teed up three or four balls at a time and whacked them as hard as I could, to try to figure out how the wind and grass would screw with them.

During the evenings I would walk the streets and look into the windows of bars, laundries and souvenir stores. I would eat bacon, bangers, fried eggs, hash browns and baked beans. In a few pubs I chowed down on mystery-meat sandwiches with curious sauces and weird veggies. One evening I dined at an Indian restaurant and nearly needed to go to the hospital for treatment of third-degree burns in my stomach.

Then I started making my suite look a bit more like an American hotel and trying to figure out where everything was. I began by stocking the refrigerator with snacks and drinks and getting soft toilet tissue for the washroom. I bought light bulbs that actually illuminated the room and then I got big bars of soap so we wouldn't have to use the puny kind the hotel provided. I bought sturdy plastic clothes hangers to add to the sole wire weakling hanging in the closet. I wondered how come the management thought it was OK to short their guests on hangers, and on towels and washcloths. I had to go out and buy *those*, too.

But I was ready for Lorna, and that was the main thing.

39

I didn't want to sound like a wimp or crybaby, but I yelled out, "Who the fuck can play in this rain and wind?"

Jake Grimsley said afterwards, "Pretty crazy weather! My cap blew off and my hair got all messed up."

Gil Donaldo said, "Great for flying kites, but not golf."

"This little guy stayed on my head the whole time," I said, tugging on the bill of my cashmere checkered cap. "You can get one in the exhibition tent for a couple of thousand dollars. They're more expensive than Bijan in there."

We loved to joke about the prices in that tent. Years earlier, we could go into the tent and find good deals, but no longer. The people who ran the businesses in the tent figured out how well cashmere sold.

I had gotten bored with the tent. Some genius had told them to shitcan the fun stuff like tractors, speedboats and sports cars and golf carts, driving nets, weird putting devices, antique jewelry, gems, silver ornaments, paintings and rare books. But no more; they had remade the tent into an oversized golf shop, and I had already been in a few hundred of those.

After the round, a few of us had a pint in the Carnoustie's ground-floor bar. We'd shed our wet clothes and changed into dry woolens. I felt quite comfy but wished my beer was a bit colder.

Gil Donaldo said, "All we can do is laugh about today. The sky was purple, the rain was coming down in sheets and I'm about to croak from hypothermia. But to the Scots it's just 'a bit of weather.' They probably think we're pussies for bitching about it so much."

Jake Grimsley said, "Tell Grover what Lance Priklan said about it."

Gil said, "Lance shook his head and said, 'Who ordered in the wind and rain machines?'"

They both laughed.

"You guys," I said, "shouldn't make sport of him like that. He may be my future stepson."

Gil Donaldo said, "Your future stepson must find it difficult going through life looking like a cover boy for a surfing magazine."

"The boy don't surf."

"Why the fuck not?" asked Gil Donaldo.

"I'm sure he could learn, but his thing is golf. Lorna says he doesn't even go to the beach to get girls."

Gil Donaldo said, "I guess if you look like Lance Priklan, all you'd have to do is drive to the beach, strip down to your Speedo and stand there while all the chicks are checking you out. Then you pick the one you want and drive off with her. Poor boy."

"'Poor boy' is right," Jake Grimlsey said. "Lance had a very bad day."

I nodded. "He nearly broke eighty. He hasn't struggled that much since he was ten years old. He actually burst into tears in front of me. He said he felt humiliated. He went over par right away and stayed there. He's leaving in a little while."

"He'll be back," said Jake Grimsley. "He'll win this thing in a few years."

"Right now, he's in his room," I told them. "Lorna is helping him pack. I'm having my driver take him to the airport."

Gil Donaldo, Jake Grimsley and I needed all of our wisdom and experience to get the first-round numbers that we considered entirely adequate considering the adverse conditions we faced. The three of us managed scores in the mid-70s range.

The leader up to that point, a limey named Craig Alferson, had shot even par. Even he couldn't believe it when he figured out he was leading the thing. No matter; we knew he would drop off the board and go home before too long.

Lorna fixed dinner for the two of us that evening. After three days, she had made our suite into a home—rearranging things, finding a grocery store, even making friends with a few of the other people.

She made us a delicious shepherd's pie, and I ate at least half of it, then sat back and let out an enormous belch.

"Glad you liked it," she said, smiling.

After dinner we cuddled on the sofa and stared at the TV set. We had only a few channels, but it couldn't have mattered less to me. I held Lorna and told myself, repeatedly, what a lucky son of a bitch I was to have her in my life. The last thing I thought before nodding off was that British people sure had funny accents.

40

We had more wind and rain to cope with throughout the second round. The course's narrow fairways, high rough and bad bounces seemed that much more challenging.

Our Friday round took close to six hours, every minute of it wet and cold. Our long day forced us to speak to each other; my companions were Jimmy Chung from China and Manuel Torres from Mexico.

Our threesome made me consider that the British Open was like a United Nations meeting, with players from all over the world, including people from countries where day-to-day survival was such an uncertain thing that one would not have guessed anybody would have the time or luxury to worry about golf.

Fifteen years ago, I debuted at the British Open. I felt a child's eagerness to see the opening ceremony and be at tee number one at seven in the morning before the first group went off in the opening round. But then, the day before the opening ceremony, I happened to be in the clubhouse at the same time as Dobie Peters, a renowned British golf writer who sat drinking a large glass of ale even though it was well before noon.

Peters overheard me talking about my desire to be out there first thing in the morning. He asked, "Why do you want to do that?"

"So I can watch the opening ceremony," I told him. "I want to be there to hear the band play and see the flags get raised and I want to listen to the officials' important remarks. Doesn't that happen on opening day?"

"Absolutely not," he said.

"Then what *does* happen?"

He shrugged. "I guess the official looks at his watch and says to the Third World golfer, 'All right, have at it.'"

We had a long delay at the 6th hole, the par-five that that had an out-of-bounds area at the left. As other guys searched around for their balls, I said to Everett, "Don't know if this is going to be the major I actually win."

"Don't hafta be, boss," he said with a smile. "Got others comin' up. One of 'em will be it." Then, "Don't this place sort of remind you of Placid Oaks back in Bayporte?"

I nodded. "But Placid doesn't get all this wind and rain."

"Good thing, too. If it did, I wouldn't be caddyin' and you probably wouldn't be golfin'."

"If I wasn't golfing, I would probably be in prison somewhere."

Everett laughed. "Makes two of us!"

The sixth hole that day really was where I began keeping myself in that contest. Due to bad bounces, I was three over on the round after five holes. However, I drove the sixth into the wind. Really hammered the ball and got it through a narrow portion that was only a dozen yards wide or so. By far that was my best shot of the day, and I followed it with an eight-foot putt that dropped right in.

I had quite a struggle, trying to make par or better on each hole. I made my other birdie on the 14th, five football fields long but otherwise one of the more manageable holes. The brisk wind, my friend for the moment, carried the ball for many yards. That hole had circular bunkers that, from a distance, looked like big grayish eyes glowering at the player. I avoided those big evil eyes and ended up with a birdie putt of six feet, an easy enough tap-in on most occasions; alas, with the wind trying to blow me off balance, I had to stand over my ball for some time before the wind died down enough for me to sink my putt.

My one-over 72 put in me a five-way tie for the lead. Normally, such a score would be nothing to feel optimistic about, but there was very little normal about this course.

"So many of you boys could win this," observed Everett. "Tiger, Ferret, Jake, Gil, a bunch of others— time you got down to business and jumped ahead of 'em all, boss."

Lorna and I dined later on at a place where they served breakfast for dinner, so I devoured a plate of eggs, bacon and potatoes. We sat where we could see the TV. We watched highlights of the day's golf. They showed me for about three seconds, wind-whipped as I tried to groove my swing. The limey doing the voiceover called me "a longtime American golfer."

Lorna laughed, shaking her head. "Those Brits. They need to do their homework. They didn't mention your name, and you're not even American."

"You know what I most love about owning an iPad? Reading the English and Scots online news services, especially when I'm here. They're so much fun. The media here don't let the facts get in the way of their telling a crackling good story. Plus, they have nudity in the news services. Know who I saw in there this morning? Soviette. I'm not sure why, but there she was. I think she was wishing us all good luck, seeing how she's engaged or married to Thom Knutson."

"I hear she's quite sexually liberated," Lorna said. "Has she ever shagged you?"

"No. Gee, I guess I'm just not very attractive."

41

On Saturday, we played the third round, and the weather, for the time being, had backed off with its attitude. We enjoyed a light breeze, and the sun even poked its way through for minutes at a time. That's why I was able to make Carnoustie my bitch.

My three-under 68 was a very low score, but a few other players had identical ones; fortunately, they were in the middle of the pack, so their low scores really didn't help them much.

My score allowed me to remain a sharp pain in the ass of Craig Alferson, the current leader, who hadn't yet caved in and fucked off.

Craig shot a 69 but teeing up his balls and hitting them longer and straighter than he should have been able to do, sinking half a dozen putts from twenty yards away for pars and birdies, and enjoying a favorable ruling from an inebriated official that enabled Craig to make a par. The official was so gooned that he allowed Craig to dig his ball out of some thick brush and put it back on the fairway at the 15th hole.

The official ruled, ludicrously, that a TV tower that interfered with Craig's line of sight. Craig later shrugged and admitted that he had asked for relief he neither deserved nor expected to receive. When the desired relief became his, nobody blamed him for accepting it.

"The wooling is yours," said the official, weaving from side to side on TV and having much difficulty making his brain and mouth work together. "TV towah block you, so you get to place yo' ball over here."

The stoned official, I noted, was Morrison Weatherby Dupree.

The reason I played well, I told the reporters, was that I managed to stay out of the heather. That beautiful stuff was a nightmare to cope with when one's ball landed in it.

I made five birdies and two bogeys. Those bogeys happened because of deep bunkers that affected other players more than they did me. I made a twenty-foot putt for birdie and did a little dance that did not end up on TV.

Lorna followed me throughout the day, impossible to miss in my gallery. Looking way too sexy in her navy turtleneck, gray slacks, black boots and mirrored sunglasses. Her long, dark hair blew about in the summer breeze as if she were in a shampoo commercial.

Everyone should have known that Lorna was checking *me* out. Who else would she be watching? Ferret Chalmers? Uh, I don't think so.

Regrettably, no writer asked me about her. I would have said something like, "Oh, her? She's some American golf groupie who's been stalking me. I don't what her problem is or what she wants with me."

Back at our hotel, Lorna took a hot bath. I napped; I'm blessed in the sense that sleep has always come easily to me. Insomnia has never tried to fuck with me, even on the night before something big. After her bath, she shook me awake and I had mine while she smoked and stared at the TV set. Afterwards I made us cocktails—a screwdriver for her and a Canadian Comfort over ice for myself—and we took our drinks with us as we went downstairs to see the owner of the inn, who had insisted that we join her for dinner.

"I see you've brought beverages," she said. "Ordinarily I don't allow alcohol here, but I'll overlook it this time." Then, "I've set out some smoked salmon and toast for you to enjoy. I'm cooking liver and onions."

Liver and onions! I shook my head at Lorna, my eyes wide with terror. My mum had made me eat that shit when I was a child, and it remained one of the most traumatic experiences of my life.

Lorna called out to our hostess, "Madam, we're awfully sorry but we have another dinner commitment elsewhere, so I'm afraid we'll have to reschedule this for another time."

The old woman said she understood, but insisted that we take some of her cooking back to our suite to enjoy later. Within minutes, we said goodnight, loaded down with a couple of platters of authentic Scots cooking along with our bottles of booze and juice. Minutes after that, we dumped the grub into the toilet and smiled with the profoundest relief.

"Liver and onions," I muttered. "In prison, they should serve that gruel three times a day. That would be a huge deterrent to criminal activity."

42

A few splashes of Canadian Comfort over ice followed by a couple of Tylenol 3s made me sleep like a dead man, but I still woke up bitchy. The liver and onions was still on my mind. When I awoke on Sunday morning, still happily buzzed on alcohol and codeine, what I thought was: If I had eaten that big meal the old woman had insisted I take home with me, what would have happened? I'd have puked; instead of sleeping in a deep, chemically induced stupor, I would have driven the porcelain bus all night and been too tired to participate the next day in a tournament I had a reasonable chance of winning.

Lorna fixed us a huge brunch of eggs, sausage, potatoes, bacon, toast and good American coffee, as opposed to muddy limey java.

I looked out the window and could see the sun, but the wind was whipping everything around. I liked that; it meant Mother Nature would keep things difficult for the superstars in the tournament. Those who were five or ten strokes behind me would stay pretty much where they were.

I had agreed to meet up with Everett at one in the afternoon and tee off at two, which gave me a few hours to watch some of the action on TV and tap on my iPad to get the American and Canadian news services.

I still couldn't decide if I liked iPads even though they didn't leave inky smudges on my fingers, and I couldn't find much in those news services about a veteran golfer from Canada who was doing big things here across the pond.

Instead, they wrote about Craig Alferson, the young Brit who was the only potential golf star England had produced in years. Here he was, a native son in a tournament on home soil. Truly an inspiring story.

Craig, indeed, was a socialite—or at least the British press said so. He was upper class, though not royalty; it meant that his family had money and his father was something better than a taxi driver. I have always admired the Brits for having a class system in which some folks are openly and officially recognized as being superior to others. In Canada and the States, we lie to each other that everyone is equal, when we clearly live in a plutocracy.

Craig, in his mid-20s, had grown up in one of London's more affluent suburbs; his father drove to and from work in a Mercedes. His father managed a firm in London that pretended to look busy.

His mum, Adelaide, went shopping most days at Harrod's and the other fancy places. Craig's younger brother, Scott, liked breaking into their neighbors' houses. His sister Allison, in her words, was a "party girl."

A relative latecomer to golf—he had taken it up in his middle teens—Craig had pondered his future, considered his father's profession boring and pointless and resolved to distinguish himself in athletics of some kind. But which sport? He lacked the speed for soccer or tennis; he was too weak for rowing and too lazy to lift weights and develop the strength necessary for such an undertaking; he was too afraid of water for swimming and wouldn't go near a horse because of what had happened to Christopher Reeve. Winter sports meant being out in the cold, and he had far too much common sense to get behind the wheel of a race car. Golfing seemed to be his only option.

Craig turned pro because he had won zero as a junior or adult amateur, and one hated to think of himself as an amateur anyway, so if he was going to keep losing, he might as well do so as a professional. He had been playing in the European Tour for the past few years without winning a dime, though he already had enough money to last a few lifetimes. His biggest payday as a golfer was little more than chump change he had picked up at some obscure tournament. He was virtually unknown as golfers went, and those who knew of him thought of him as the rich British lad with nothing better to do than play bad golf all day. He had almost missed the cut for the British Open.

Asked about his current struggle, Craig said, "Every course is hard, right? You hit the ball, and either it goes in the right direction or it goes somewhere else. The ball seems to have a bloody mind of its own, doesn't it?"

Of all those guys on the course playing ahead of Craig and me, none had made much progress in catching up with me by the time we teed off.

One reason was that the course had copped an attitude. Its grass had gotten dry and the winds now came from different directions, sometimes helping the golfer, other times infuriating him. The balls went farther and higher sometimes, which was not always a good thing.

We began with the appearance of official-looking folks in dark jackets and media people covering the event for their countries; after all, this was the final round of the British Open, so there needed to be some pomp and circumstance.

One of the guys in dark jackets, James Morrison Weatherby Dupree, had arrived as a guest of some kind. That fucker had the audacity to give me a big, toothy smile and go-get-'em fist pump just before I teed up.

What the fuck? Did he think we were a couple of old pals from the other side of the world who needed to stick together in this foreign land? Did he think I wouldn't still be angry at him because of the way he'd fucked me over at the Masters and U.S. Open? He'd only been doing his job; no hard feelings? Surely I was a big enough man to understand?

I stared at him and gave him the tiniest of nods. Good manners die hard.

I had on a navy golf shirt with light-gray slacks and black golf shoes. Craig wore a white golf shirt under an argyle sleeveless sweater and navy slacks. His shoes were gleaming burgundy.

When teeing up on this course, I knew enough to make sure that I kept my ball on the fairway. I told Craig so, but he seemed indifferent to my advice. He had found his own creative way to play.

The first hole, a couple of football fields long, was a simple enough par-four. I teed off, hit my ball hard and it landed in the middle of the fairway. From there I reached the pin with two shots. Nice for me.

Craig, however, whacked his ball straight into the rough and had a long, difficult shot to make it to the green. He made it. More than that, he sank a 40-foot putt that nearly made me cry. As Everett and I walked along to the next tee, I said, "That laddy is starting to look like a real golfer."

Over the next eight holes, I played the most efficient and disciplined golf of my entire life. Each drive ended up on the fairway, and each shot or two from there ended up on the green. My putts sank, almost without exception.

Ordinarily, I would have daydreamed about the wonderful things I'd be reading about myself on my iPad: Canada'a Grover Bobbitt wins British Open and would have gazed, with much love and admiration, at the online image at myself holding the trophy.

But that good shit did not happen. What *did* happen was that despite my excellent performance, Craig's goofy, inept drives and shots kept going where they were supposed to be. On one hole after another, he teed off and got into trouble, then hit his ball stupidly and angrily and ended up on the fairway. Again and again he sank miraculous putts although, judging by his technique, I would say he didn't know *how* to putt.

The Brits behind the rope cheered, whistled and screamed each time one of Craig's clumsy shots turned out well.

In the moments when I made eye contact with Lorna, I could only roll my eyes and run a frustrated hand through my hair.

As we walked to the back nine, Everett said, "What we have here is a big problem. That Craig? When it comes to golf, he don't even know what he don't know. But he got Lady Luck on his side, and no golfer alive can beat *that* bitch."

43

As much as I love golf lore, I have never wanted to become part of it. I love jokes, too—love to hear them, tell them, laugh at them. Just so long as I'm not the joke.

My drive at the 10th was not the stuff of lore. I ended up in the rough, but the rough was low because hundreds of fans had trampled on it. I thought I could whack the ball hard enough to get it out of the rough and onto the green.

Alas. I knew as I swung that I hadn't hit it nearly hard enough. At the same time, that son of a bitch Craig made it onto the green with two shots, and my job then became to make sure my performance on that hole didn't become a disaster, or at least a bigger disaster. I was thinking, 'Well, maybe I'll end up with a double bogey and he'll make par. Oh, well. This tournament isn't over till it's over.'

Throughout my struggle, Craig kept sinking crucial putts and generally playing well.

We both parred one hole after another, and Craig ended up on the 18th tee, par four, over 400 yards. Plenty of dangerous places on that hole, but he avoided them all and made par, which gave him a three-shot lead, and *that* gave him a good enough score to win probably the first thing of significance in his entire overprivileged, underachieving life, which was the British Open.

44

Zillions of limey fans cheered and applauded, as if Prince Wils or Harry had just come out to wave hidy. The fans then took him upon their shoulders and sang and cried and carried on as if he'd just saved the queen or something.

Lorna stood waiting for me as I emerged from the scorer's tent. We grabbed onto each other, rubbed noses, kissed and I tried not to cry, which was easy enough because I'm just not a crier. We watched the fans as they carried on over Craig's victory; even though he was a limey, for the moment the Scots were claiming him as one of their own.

Those Scots always weirded me out. I had known a few who seemed genuinely good-natured, but mostly the Scots struck me as pig-headed folks who took pride in their hatred of the British and Americans. They hated the Brits for a dozen reasons, and hated the Americans because, back in 1939, Roosevelt wouldn't send U.S. troops to help the Brits fight off the Nazis.

"You played great," Lorna said. "I was so proud of you."

"I played my best," I told her. "It wasn't good enough."

She shook her head. "That guy Craig. He's such a doofus. He hardly knows which end of the club to hold."

"Well, he knew enough today. I still can't believe some of the putts he sank."

"Yeah, I kept expecting him to goof up and have some bad rounds. But it didn't happen."

"It wasn't meant to be for me, sweetie," I told her. "But I'm no loser. How can I be a loser if I'm standing here with you in my arms?"

"You're so wonderful," she murmured.

"I've been thinking about something," I said. "All my life, I've put most of my energy into golf. It's been my obsession. I've studied how to golf, when to golf, which kinds of equipment—every aspect of the game. I play all the time and have made enough money at it to live in comfort, but I've never gotten what I really want, which is to win a major. Well, I've finally learned the main thing. It doesn't matter how expensive your equipment is or how often you try new swings. The main thing, the thing that really matters, is psychological. The thing that matters is how you cope with the setbacks, the bad rulings, the disappointments."

PART FOUR

45

Before heading back to North America, I promised Lorna I would take her to London for a week. I would pay for it with the fistful of money I had won for coming in second in Scotland.

Well, London wasn't that expensive, and I say that because I had been to some of the world's most expensive cities and London was no costlier than those other places.

Sometimes, if you're as obtuse as I am, you take a very long while to figure out that walking is often the best and most efficient way of getting around in London. Taxis take forever because of all the one-way streets, and I've stood on the sidewalk and looked on with amazement at how eight zillion vehicles creep along each day. It's worse than New York.

If you're totally ignorant of London's layout, you may step outside your hotel's front door, hail a taxi and give him your destination. Instead of saying, "You would be better off walking—that's just three blocks away," the driver takes you halfway across the city before finally depositing you at the place you wanted to go to. Everyone's got some sort of hustle going.

Well, I didn't do much of that; instead, I ate, slept, read the online news services on my iPad and watched British TV. I said to myself, 'I think they're speaking English but I can't understand a word of it.'

Lorna and I went for walks. We strolled through parks and stared at statues. Looking at those edifices, I felt the same indifference to England's heroes that I assumed limeys felt when they went to the States and saw the Statue of Liberty or the Vietnam Veterans' Memorial.

On my previous visits to London I had come to love the places where they served me a delicious plate of roast beef and Yorkshire pudding, just as Jews in New York cherish the places that serve great kosher food.

But Lorna had this retarded guide to dining in London, and all the eateries she dragged me into had no roast beef and Yorkshire pudding. Our server often brought us something that still had a pulse.

Lorna insisted that we go to the theatre. She said it would expand my horizons. I told her I was just a hick from Canada who wanted to keep his horizons nice and narrow.

The three of us—Lorna, me and her American Express card—went shopping at Debenhams, Harrods, Fortnum and Mason and a dozen other stores.

I said, "Don't go into Harrods right now. It's the hottest July they've had in s long time, the store has its sales on, so it will be crowded, and you'll be totally miserable."

"Don't worry about me," she replied. "I'm from California. I know how to function in hot weather."

"Well," I said, "London hot weather is different from other kinds of hot weather."

But off she went. I waited for her in a coffee shop across the street. After half an hour, she traipsed out of there and across the street, looking half dead. When she got to the coffee shop, she plopped down into the chair across from me and ran a hand through her limp, greasy hair.

"God," she muttered, "that was fucking awful."

Lorna stayed with me in Bayporte for several days before flying back to southern California. She'd decided that an office for International Athletic Management my city might be a feasible thing after all. She checked out rents and leases in case she decided to accept her ex's offer to run the agency's as-yet-uncreated satellite office.

"I think you should get something near the harbor. It's nice to look out the window and see the water," I told her.

"I don't much care what you think," she told me.

Lorna wondered just how much space she would need. "Probably four or five room," she said. "One for me, another for a receptionist, one for a flunky and the last one for a computer geek."

"Why a geek?" I asked.

"Because," she told me, "I've learned from dealing with my son that nearly all professional golfers—and, I suppose, most professional athletes—are hopelessly inept at everything except playing sports."

"You speak the truth," I told her.

"Travel, lodging, homes, insurance, taxes, investments, savings, expenses, doctors? They need help with *all* that shit. That's why there are agents. We help them with those everyday things that ordinary people deal with."

"And God bless ya for doing it," I said. "I think you'll be a better agent than my guy, Barney Smoltz."

"If I accept Bruce's offer to join his agency, maybe we'll bring Barney aboard."

I nodded. "He's a whore. He's for sale."

Lorna looked only at the inner city for office space, and she liked the fact that a trip from downtown to the airport would take only an hour, if that long. She narrowed it down to two properties: the Bayporte Club on Grand Street and the Nu West Sports skyscraper. The two ugliest buildings in the world, according to Gil Donaldo, that esteemed architecture critic.

The first Canadian reporter to bug me for an interview once I got home was Clancy Wasserman from *Canadian Sports Online*. I took him to lunch at Julio's so I could watch him devour a huge plate of Mexican food and wash it down with a half-dozen margaritas.

He got sufficiently gooned and told me things I already knew but enjoyed hearing anyway. "My boss wouldn't ley me go to the British Open with you guys, and I'm still mad about it. He said, 'The Open happens just when the Invaders are getting ready for training camp.' Of course, that bloody training camp must be the most important thing in the world to the fools who edit that rag. I mean, a nine-point-nine earthquake could make California break into one huge piece and float away into the ocean, but that earthquake would a page-two story if one of the Bayporte Invaders got a hemorrhoid."

Clancy mostly updated the feature story he had written about me for the past half-dozen years: Bayporte' Grover Bobbitt remains one of professional golf's top players and money winners. This time he added the stuff about how I was a runner-up twice overseas and pocketed some big cash as a result. He made it sound like I was thrilled to get what I'd gotten.

I disliked the headline, too: "Grover Bobbitt Comes Close Twice."

Fuck you very much, I thought.

Winnie Ellerd, the chick reporter from *Bayporte Sports* magazine, called me to ask a question: What did I think of Marni Sandusky's press conference?

"What did she say?" I asked.

"She said she would shoot herself in the head on the golf course at Oakland Hills during the PGA Championship unless they changed their membership policy."

"Committing suicide, eh? Was that a threat or a promise?"

"Don't be a smartass, Grover."

"What is Marni's problem now? What is she complaining about? She must know that Oakland Hills accepts women, too."

"She does. She says they don't have enough pretty ones there."

"What?"

"Just kidding. She says they have too many Caucasian gentiles at Oak Park."

"That's another joke, right?"

"Wrong. Marni doesn't seem to realize what an idiot she is. She says, 'Every woman in America owes her career to what I've accomplished on behalf of women everywhere.' She thinks I should thank her for my job, too."

"Oh? Have you spoken to her?"

"Yeah, on the phone. I felt like saying, 'If you're so interested in my career because I'm a woman, maybe you should bug *Sports Illustrated* to hire me away from this shitty *West Coast Golf* gig.'"

"Did Marni say specifically where and when she would blow her brains out?"

"No. Does it turn you on a little bit?"

"Yes, it does. I'd just like to know where she's gonna be when she puts a bullet through her skull. My ball might get stuck in her blood."

"That's an awful thing to say. I love it."

"You know, Clancy Wasserman is still pissed off that *CS* didn't send him to cover the Open," I told her.

"Yeah, I was disappointed that *my* boss kept me home, too. They said they needed me here more than there. What a pisser!"

"Hard luck," I said.

46

My mum and dad invited us over for dinner so they could meet Lorna. Well, actually, they had met her before, but I think my dad had a boner for her and wanted to see her again before she flew back to sunny California. We had salmon steaks, corn on the cob, asparagus with hollandaise sauce and white wine from a local vineyard.

"Here in Canada," my dad told Lorna, "we're all about meat. Fish, fowl, beef, pork—we love it all. If you ask me, vegetarians are idiots. They don't know what they're missing."

"I think they believe that meat is full of carcinogens and that animals are treated with the utmost cruelty before they're killed and processed into food," Lorna said.

"Too bad," said my dad.

"Did you go to war?" Lorna asked.

"Sure did. Korea. Would have gone to Vietnam, too, but Canada wasn't involved in it."

"Who was your favorite prime minister?"

He shrugged. "Don't have one. They're all the same to me."

"Got a favorite president?"

"Certainly not Barack Obama."

"Why not?"

"Because he's much ado about nothing. When he was elected, black people said, 'I wept because one of our own finally became president.' Well, not exactly. Obama is mulatto, not black. Also, he was the Harvard-educated junior senator from Illinois before he came president, so he's every bit as much a big-government politician as all the others whom black America considers the enemy. Nothing's gonna change with him or any of the other Democrats or Republicans who move into the White House in the years ahead."

"What did you think of Ike Eisenhower?" she asked.

"He was a good guy, but he was such a Republican. When he was in office, a man couldn't get a loan from a bank unless he could prove he didn't need it. My, how times have changed."

"How about Kennedy?"

"Handsome man. Sharp dresser."

"LBJ?"

"The Vietnam president. He was so worried about his public image that he was afraid to act on Vietnam for fear he would make a bad decision. So, by doing nothing, he became one of the biggest fools ever to occupy the White House."

"How about Nixon?"

"Didn't have an ethical bone in his body. Deserved what he got."

"Gerald Ford?"

"First thing he did was to pardon Nixon."

"Jimmy Carter?"

"First thing *he* did was to pardon the draft dodgers. He would have gotten my vote—for parson. But the job of president requires brains, brawn and balls, and I'm afraid Carter was singularly lacking in all three."

"How about Reagan?"

"He slept through most of his two terms. His aides said he snoozed during meetings, and that delighted me. I've always said that the president does best who does least."

"George Bush?"

"Damn good man, damn good American. Just too bad he didn't get his second term. Slick Willie got that."

"And what of Slick Willie?"

"He did absolutely, positively jackshit, which of course was a good thing. Well, he did get impeached, which was not altogether a good thing. Now he practices law in Harlem and pretends that he did a good job in the White House. But does he really go into Harlem and practice law five days a week or does he just keep an office there so he'll have a relatively cheap Manhattan business address?"

"How about Dubya?"

"Recovering alcoholic who, despite his master's degree in business administration from Harvard, went back home to Texas and lost millions due to making spectacularly poor oil-drilling decisions. Not half as good a president as his daddy was, but much better than many others."

"Are you optimistic about the future?"

He shook his head. "No, but I'm an old man. The future isn't mine to worry about."

47

Throughout my life, I have loved movies, especially the ones in which two desirable women verbally fight over some handsome man who dresses well and smokes cigarettes. He never seems to have a job and it's the middle of the Great Depression, but so what?

When I was a younger movie freak, I thought I would have lots of fun being that guy the women fought over, particularly if one of those women was Ingrid Bergman, for whom I was insanely horny. But then I heard my mum and dad talk about heating and air conditioning back then, and a hundred other things I couldn't have lived without, and I mostly stopped having those fantasies about being a Depression-era ladies' man.

Still, I had that fantasy on the day I arranged to have lunch with my two best gals, Lorna and Simone Allerd, at Placid Oaks Country Club. Both ladies were Ingrid Bergman to me. OK, maybe I pretended one or the other was Cyd Charisse. I'd always had a boner for Cyd, too.

I couldn't be their leading man and mutual love interest because that man always smoked, and I didn't smoke, and couldn't have smoked even if I'd wanted to do so. The Bayporte lawmakers had made cigarettes almost as illegal as PCP.

We sat in the dining room that had huge windows overlooking the golf course, as if watching the players were part of the entertainment. I nodded and smiled at the other people in the dining room; they were dressed in everything from tennis togs to pinstriped suits.

A member came to our table. "I saw you at the British Open. You made me proud to be a Canadian. That guy who won? Greg All-for-none or whatever his name is? I can't believe he won the thing. Can you?"

I just shook my head.

"When's the next PGA?" he asked.

"Couple of weeks," I told him.

"Gonna be there?"

Well, duh. It would be the last major of the year, in August, the time of stifling heat, football season approaching, the baseball pennant races. The PGA Championship is nobody's idea of golf's most prestigious major, and that's too bad.

"Yeah," I told the guy, "I'll be there."

"Well," he said, "just don't fuck up."

"I'll try not to."

He went away, and I suddenly got the feeling that, in this well-populated room, people I did not know staring at me, probably thinking, 'How can that goof be with those two beautiful women? Who the fuck does he think he is? Who the fuck do *they* think he is?'

Naturally, I felt delighted to have two lovelies as my lunch companions, even if I just sat there eating and listening as they talked about how, while they ran their own businesses, what they *really* did was pay way too fucking much in taxes.

"Sounds like you two have plenty in common," I said. "That pleases me."

They blew me off with tiny sneers and went on rapping about chick stuff.

"I don't like hiring surfer girls," Lorna said. "If the waves are good, they'll call in sick. Hitting the beach and getting tanned are their top priorities in life."

"I hate putting up 'help wanted' signs," said Simone. "I mean, you can't *imagine* what kind of riff raff comes in and wants to apply for a job."

"Oh, yes I can," retorted Lorna, and they both howled.

I said, "Los Angeles has more Canadians than any city outside of Canada. California has a larger population than Canada."

They both snarled at me.

Later on, after the chicks had stopped rapping, I asked Simone a question.

"Have you heard from Helene at all? Any idea what kind of crazy nonsense she's up to?"

Lorna said, "You mean your third wife?"

I nodded.

Simone chuckled. "No, I don't stay in touch with her, but I hear she's doing better every day. I understand she bought one of the bigger mansions in West Shore. I've been in one or two of those houses. They all have terrific views. From the terrace you can see Hong Kong.

"Anyway, not long ago we got a gig to provide the yummies at a luncheon for rich ladies. Well, it seems that Helene is now dating Laddy Froman, a short fat goof who's in his sixties. Everyone laughs at him behind his back. He hasn't worked in years, if ever; he gets by on an inheritance. For years he'd impressed people with the fact that his great-great-grandfather or someone was Abe Froman, one of Great Elizabeth's first premiers. Laddy liked to go away on weekends and come back wearing casts and braces and whatever and say that he had hurt himself playing polo or something. But everyone said, 'Yeah, Laddy, sure,' because they knew if he had been injured, it was probably from playing bum-touch football with six-year-old boys.

"Those rich ladies thought it would be a good idea for Helene to marry Laddy Froman because she thinks he is rich and socially influential. Those ladies wouldn't be at all surprised if Laddy tried to marry Helene—after all, he's a sixty-something bachelor and if he got married, people might stop thinking of him as a pederast."

"Those two deserve each other," I said.

At the end of lunch, Simone said, "Lorna, are you going to the PGA in Detroit?"

"Not sure yet. I haven't been to my gallery in a few weeks. I have to go home at some point and make sure my business partner hasn't ripped me off. But I'll probably get to the PGA because my two best fellas will be there."

"I envy you," Simone said. "Your son is becoming a superstar golfer. It must be fun for you, watching him do his thing."

"It terrifies me. *He* terrifies me." Lorna shuddered. "Lance gets so cocky sometimes. It's like he wants me to have a heart attack out there."

"Lorna," Simone said, "I feel as if you and I are already friends, so would you mind if I asked you a very personal question?"

Lorna shrugged. "Ask."

"What, exactly, do you want with my ex?"

Lorna shot a look at me and said, "He's the best guy I've known in quite a while. I want to spend as much time as possible with him...for as long as possible."

Simone smiled. "Good to know. He hasn't been with many women who were worthy of him."

"He was with you," Lorna said.

"Yeah, but we weren't ready for each other. We still had too much growing up yet to do. After me, of course, he took up with Hell-een."

Simone smiled some more. "I have to tell you how amazing you two are, staying friends after your divorce. It's very unselfish and generous and mature. It doesn't happen everywhere, and it certainly doesn't happen down in sunny California, enchanted land of acrimonious divorces. I may go to work for my ex, and if I do, it will be for my son's benefit as well as my own. I will demand a salary that will make me wonderfully stinking rich. But I won't enjoy working for my ex, because I think he's an unethical son of a bitch."

"Our friendship is unusual," Simone said. "I suppose it's just Bayporte, but people here hold onto their grudges a really long time, which makes any sort of friendship between divorced couples next to impossible."

"Ladies," I said, "may I butt in for a moment?"

"Shut up," they said in unison.

48

Clark Irving's book arrived with a batch of junk mail, and I felt tempted to call his book junk mail, too. I was getting ready to head out for the PGA Championship at Oakland Hills in Detroit.

Clark had included a note:

"Grover, just between you and me, I wrote this one as fast as I could, so don't expect a masterpiece. I wanted it to be on the shelves in time for football season. It's already on the charts. Happy reading."

Typical Clark note: ME ME ME ME. I would have appreciated a missive that went, "Too bad for you at the British Open, but that's the way the ball bounces (no pun intended). Anyway, congrats on finishing second. Maybe next time, huh?" If I had won the Open, he would have said, "Write a book about it pronto, while the people out there give a shit about Grover Bobbitt. We might call it *From Bayporte to the British Open by Grover Bobbitt and Clark Irving.*" No thanks, Clark.

I put his book aside, to be donated to the Bayporte Public Library when I got around to it.

When I picked up the telephone, Vanessa was calling from Germany. Strom was sitting in their hotel room, tucking away a room-service dinner.

"We're here in Berlin because I wanted to go to one

of my favorite places from when I was a flight attendant for Canadian," she said. "I actually used to fly from Bayporte to Munich, but that's neither here nor there.

"We really like Berlin. It's a chic, fashionable city. Next we're going to Italy. We have a good suite reserved in Italy, but if it's not good enough, we'll just get something better. You can do that when you have money."

"If you say so," I told her.

"Strom is sitting right here, but he's eating like a stevedore and doesn't want his food to get cold, so he won't be coming to the phone. Are you OK with that, Grover?"

"Suits me fine," I said. "How's his golf game coming along?"

"Fine, I guess. I have some important news, and that's why I'm calling. You remember Kevin and Warren, my kids from when I was with Thom Knutson? Well, my two little stooges have gotten into trouble again, and just before they were supposed to enter college. It happened while you were in England, otherwise, you would have heard about it. Thom had to rush out to Connecticut and make the trouble go away. I guess it worked, because they didn't have to do any jail time and they got to enroll at Bellis College, just as we'd planned."

"I'll bet Thom had to write a few checks," I said.

"Oh, sure. It cost him some megabucks, but he can afford it." She paused. "Actually, I'm disappointed that the two stooges didn't have to do the time. I really think they would have benefited from incarceration, and the rest of us would have been better off with the stooges locked up for a while. It galls me that they just wreak havoc and get to walk away from it."

"Tell me *specifically* what your stooges did this time," I said.

"Well," Vanessa said, taking a deep breath, "Kevin and Warren had gone out to have a look at Bellis College before actually starting classes there. While they were checking out the town and campus, they encountered two empty golf carts that belonged to workers who were doing renovations at a nearby apartment complex.

"So, you *know* how much my boys like their fun. They got into the carts and decided to have a race."

"Uh oh," I said.

"I'm not sure it was anyone's fault that by the time they reached the top of a hill, they lost control of the carts. Anyway, there they were, going downhill at fifty miles per hour and no way of stopping. Fortunately, they were able to jump out before the carts crashed through the window of a daycare center."

"How many casualties?"

"Oh, no one was killed."

"Good to know," I said.

"But a few kids and some adults had to be hospitalized. The adults were screaming, 'I'll sue! I'll sue!' but then Thom arrived and whipped out his checkbook. He said. 'OK, how much do you want?' That made the problem go away."

"I'll bet it did."

I felt relieved that Kevin and Warren hadn't killed anyone yet, but I felt even better when I learned that Gil Donaldo had won his first major. I cheered for him from my living room TV at home in Bayporte before flying out to Detroit for the PGA.

Gil had won the Firestone in Akron, Ohio, by half a dozen strokes. When we met up in Detroit, I asked, "How does it feel being a millionaire?"

He shrugged. "I won't be one for long. I have a mountain of bills to pay."

Gil Donaldo, Jake Grimsley and I stayed at the Doubletree, along with a number of other players, including Lance Priklan. His mother, Lorna, would be flying out to join us in a day or two. She had stayed in some modest hotels in her life, and some shabby ones, and she said she liked the fancy ones best. I knew she would be happy in the Doubletree because it was among the swankiest I had ever seen, at least in Detroit.

The room I'd reserved for us was the Bridal Suite. Funny thing was, Lorna and I weren't getting married, at least not then. Thom Knutson and Soviette were.

49

"Gil," I asked, "would you rather have your wedding in Las Vegas, being married by an Elvis impersonator, or would you rather write your own vows, invite the public and get married on a soundstage during a golf match?"

"Both choices suck," he replied.

Thom and Soviette went for the soundstage, which was under a tent, and the tent sat on the easier of Oakland Hills' two courses. The bosses at Oakland Hills always used their more difficult course for major tournaments and temporarily converted into a soundstage for putting on concerts for the many folks who had no clubhouse access. Next to the soundstage, a merchandise tent sold every kind of junk a golfer or golf fan.

Thom and Soviette's wedding happened on the soundstage as, outside, the Midwestern sky darkened into a marvelous azure on the evening before the tournament. Lorna and I stood way in the back of the vast tent as the sound system boomed the couple's vows probably all the way up to Canada. They could have aired out the place a bit more; the people sitting near me were all funky from being out in the muggy Detroit heat all day. I'd been to petting zoos that smelled fresher.

I stood there with Lorna, Gil Donaldo and Jake Grimsley. Lorna had flown up that day from Florida, where she'd helped Lance turn his condo or townhouse into a pussy trap. He had been practicing for the tournament, just like the rest of us.

Lance, to his credit, had taken a pass on the wedding. At that moment, he and his father were in downtown Detroit, having a lavish dinner with Hana Palmer, the fifteen-year-old girl stud golfer who had recently signed with Bruce Priklan's agency.

Bruce Priklan didn't fuck around. I respected him for that. One of his first duties as Hana Palmer's agent was to line up a deal for her to cover this golf event for CBS. She would walk with us, interview us and summarize the action for the TV audience.

What did the network care that she knew zero about men's golf or Oakland Hills? She was pretty and poised; the mostly male viewers could fixate on her cute face and dimpled smile as they masturbated.

"I notice that Marni Sandusky isn't here," I said to Lorna.

"Gee, that's too bad."

"I guess now there will be nobody to object when the preacher asks, 'Is there anyone here…?'"

Lorna shrugged. "Maybe she's just saving her disruptive energies for later."

One could say with confidence that freak-show fans outnumbered well-wishers at Thom and Soviette's wedding. They had two obscure heavy metal bands playing, each doing a brief set that sounded like a very long one, and they couldn't have sounded worse if they had played at the same time, or if each member of each band had been playing a different song, which perhaps they did. Personally, I thought that Metallica, Megadeth, Judas Priest, Slayer, Iron Maiden and all the others sounded alike. I wanted to leave the moment the first band clambered onto the stage, but Lorna and the others insisted that I stick around and endure the entertainment.

By and by the bride and groom appeared, both dressed in virginal white. She emerged from the left wing of the stage and he from the right. At the center, they clasped hands, faced the crowd and bowed. Everyone cheered, whistled and applauded.

Soviette thanked the two bands for trying to entertain us. "So good, so good! Check them out on YouTube! Give them a 'like'!"

She then said she wanted to thank all of her own fans who had shown her so much support. Lorna caught me rolling my eyes and gave me a gentle elbow in the ribs.

"This," she whispered to me, "is one of the worst ideas ever."

"You mean even worse than diet pop?"

"Almost but not quite."

As Thom stood onstage beaming and nodding at everything Soviette said, "I have prayed to God about how to marry the man I love, and He said, 'Girl, you don't need a minister. Just do it from the heart and I'll accept it.' So that's what we're going to do."

And here is how they did it:

Soviette: "Tommy-Boy, my big man with the three long legs, you are hardly my first but definitely my best, and I am committed to you for the rest of my life."

Tommy-Boy: "Big Red, I want to keep jumping your bones and making you scream for the rest of your life."

Their dirty talk went on for some time—an hour or more, maybe longer—and we could still hear them as we, and the equally embarrassed masses, went away.

50

Throughout my first day at the PGA, I couldn't find whether or not I liked that course at Oakland Hills. Then I decided that a course was a course was a course, and the course didn't care diddly-do if I liked it or not.

On the second day, I shot well but not great; still, I was on the leaderboard and the other golfers knew damn well that Grover Bobbitt was there and he wasn't fuckin' around.

Thom Knutson, however, had left his golf game between the legs of his bride, Soviette, who had flown out to New York or L.A. to perform and be interviewed on MTV. After Soviette took off, I saw Thom by the rope, smiling at and touching the arm of Cookie, Stu Claudell's friendly wife. Presently Thom withdrew from the tournament, citing hemorrhoids or something, and disappeared with Cookie.

But this is about me, not Thom and his wandering dick. My goal was to be a major presence that day, when I knew that the last four holes would decide the winner.

Oakland Hills' last four holes, many fine golfers said, were among the most difficult they had ever encountered. They weren't easy, of course, but I found them totally playable and felt proud of myself for playing such kick-ass golf into my 40s. I knew that one of the reasons I was doing so well at my age at such a crucial tournament was that Weatherby Dupree, or whatever his name was, had not graced us with his presence. The reason for his absence was that Dupree was in a hospital somewhere waiting, in some desperation, for a double kidney transplant.

"He'd better get them soon," said Fay Dacell, the USGA boss, "or he'll be working the big green course in the sky."

"Too bad," I said.

Fay shook his head. "Dupree's wife comes from a family that's even richer than his, and despite all that money, he's at the Mayo, waiting for kidneys that may never come. I've got this jumbo get-well card"—it *was* jumbo, about two feet by four feet—"and I'd like you fellas to sign it so I can have it FedExed out to him while he's still got time to enjoy it. He's sure meant a lot to the game of golf, you know."

"Well," I replied, "he's sure meant a lot to *my* golf game."

"I know you two didn't always get along," Fay said, "but I think it would be mighty big of you to sign this card and show him there are no hard feelings."

I nodded and signed the card.

Gil Donaldo refused to sign it. "Not after the way he treated Grover. No fuckin' way."

"That's unsportsmanlike conduct," said Fay.

"So Dupree is waiting for someone to croak so he can have their kidneys?"

"Yep," said Fay.

"Tell me when a porn star dies so I can have his cock," said Gil. "As long as he was white and didn't have AIDS."

51

I kept grooming my swing on the practice range, so I missed much of the Friday-night entertainment, but when Lorna and I arrived, Marni Sandusky stood at the microphone, on the spot where Thom and Soviette had promised to love, honor and screw each other till doomsday.

"Beautiful people," Marni was shouting, "how many mulatto transgendered people have been admitted to the private golf clubs where the elite capitalist swine rule over and oppress the masses?"

"None!"

Marni went on like that for a few more minutes, ignoring the fact that maybe 30 people comprised her audience. One of those people, the reporter Winnie Ellerd, gave us an update.

"Marni decided against killing herself."

"How come?" I asked.

Lorna shot me a don't-be-an-ass look.

"She said a few minutes ago that she'd forgotten to bring her gun, and even if she'd brought it, the security people would have confiscated it. So shooting herself was not an option. Stabbing herself would have too slow; someone would have tried to save her. So, the best thing was for to stay alive and spread her message far and wide."

"So I promise you now," Marni was saying, "that wherever there are people of color being oppressed by thieving, money-hungry, exploitative white bastards, I'll be there!"

"*Yes!*"

After listening for a few more minutes, I said to Lorna, "I've heard enough of this. Let's go."

She nodded.

"So long, Mario Savio," I said as we departed.

"Who?" Lorna asked.

"The Free Speech Movement. Berkeley, Nineteen Sixty-four."

"What?"

"You've got to bone up on your Bay Area history, babe."

52

As practically everyone who paid attention to golf in particular, sports in general or popular culture knew, Lance Priklan, the stud muffin with the cover-boy looks, was getting busy to kick some ass at this tournament. As always, he was hitting the ball so far into the sky that we feared his tee balls would hit overhead aircraft.

The spectacle of Lance Priklan launching a ball into the stratosphere has often prompted Gil Donaldo to shake his head and say, "If that boy wasn't so ugly, he'd really have it made."

Lance immediately got ahead of Ferret Chalmers, Ken Duke and me. I knew I would have one fewer woman in my gallery, too.

"I'm going to root for my son," Lorna said. "No offense, Grover."

"None taken," I replied. "If he wins, give him s kiss for me. I would do it myself, but I don't think I'm his type."

Since I no longer had Lorna winking and smiling at me, I paid attention only why I was there: To win the fucking tournament. It must have been that lesson I had taught myself on the practice range: Silence the *shreck* buzzing inside my head and hit the ball. I was two under by the time I was at the final hour holes. I parred those holes, and Everett, my caddy, threw back his head and howled.

"Grover," he exclaimed, "you jes' slapped them four holes aroun' like they was yo' misbehavin' bitches."

Winnie Ellerd, the sportswriter, jumped out in front

of me as I emerged from the scorer's tent.

"Grover," she said, catching her breath, "give me a little something, just for me, before you talk to the others."

Smirking and shrugging, I said, "I went out there today with a Zen attitude. I wanted to become one with the golf course in this chaotic universe."

"Fantastic!" She squealed and poked me in the stomach, then scampered off to the press tent.

Lance Priklan, who I believed would become my son-in-law within a year, had played pretty good golf himself. He'd shot a very adequate 70 for his worldwide fan club of zillions, plus his mum, but it left him one behind his mum's squeeze.

I'd shit, showered and shaved and started trying to decide on what to wear for dinner when Barney Smoltz, my agent, called to tell me to keep up the good work. He said he was sorry that he wouldn't be able to fly out to Michigan to say hi, but he had to deal with some more bullshit involving Cartier Dymont, his NBA client.

Cartier, a Los Angeles Clippers seven-footer, had beaten a pair of rape charges earlier that year. But he'd just been busted again for allegedly abducting and raping Trudy Richmond, the pretty defense attorney who had gotten him acquitted earlier.

Trudy Richmond was ready to testify that Cartier Dymont entered her office and kidnapped her with the sight of his handgun pressed to her temple. Then he took her to his suite at the Chateau Panache, where he lived, and he chained her to his bed for three days and raped her a dozen times.

Additionally, Cartier Dymont called a teammate, Ferrari Carr, and invited him over to join the fun. Trudy Richmond couldn't be absolutely, positively sure that Ferrari Carr was the other guy because she kept losing consciousness. But, as she put it, "Who else is hung like him?"

Trudy had been saved by police after they discovered Cartier, roaring drunk and reeking of weed, staggering along Wilshire Boulevard. He was naked but for boxer shorts, sunglasses and a Clippers cap.

Barney said, "Cartier says it wasn't rape because, as he said, 'She had a itchy pussy, man. You could just tell.'"

"Charming," I said.

"You watch that court TV shit all the time, right?"

"More than I should," I told him.

"Well, would you look around and find me a criminal-defense attorney—a woman, of course—who will represent Cartier? But make sure she's no cutie like Trudy Richmond."

"Gotcha. Woman lawyer, no cutie."

"And Grover? Keep doing that Zen shit when you're on the golf course. 'I want to become one with the universe.' Sometimes you fuckin' bust my onions."

53

So Bruce Priklan got in and insisted that we all have dinner with him at some fancy restaurant near the golf course. Frankly, I didn't want to go, and neither did Lorna, Lance or Hana. But we all went anyway.

Bruce arrived in a dark suit, light shirt and sober tie. He also had on traces of makeup because he had just done a TV interview in which he predicted that Hana Palmer would become the next Caucasian female Tiger Woods. I wasn't sure who the *first* Caucasian female Tiger Woods was.

Hana arrived with Bruce. She had on tight Levi's, a light-blue T-shirt and looked like a cute kid who was enjoying all the attention everyone was giving her. Bruce looked like he owned everyone and everything but he still didn't have enough.

Hana and I hadn't seen each other in a little while, and she looked at me then looked away, as if she feared I would rush over, take her across my lap and spank her bum till it was covered with welts.

I went over and shook her hand. It wasn't her fault that she knew the rules of golf better than I did, and it made no sense to become enemies with the next Caucasian female Tiger Woods.

"You're playing good golf," she told me.

"I'm concentrating better. How do you like being on TV?"

She shrugged. "It's not glamorous. It's just walking near you guys, wearing a headset and hearing someone say, 'Be ready to make an observation when we give you your cue.' Only thing is, they rarely let me have my say."

"Well, I'm sure you'll get your turn," I told her.

"I'm not sure being a TV personality is for me," she said. "I mean, I'm like you. I *love* to play golf. I'll never get sick of it. it fits my skill set perfectly. I'm also totally competitive and love to win. It's just who I am. I couldn't imagine getting up every morning and saying, 'Oh, no! Not another day of dragging myself through a job that I hate and taking orders from bosses I want to punch out.'"

I laughed. "Yeah, that's no fun." Then, "Remember what the hippies said: 'Do your thing.' And if golf is your thing, just do it. Do it, have fun and win. If you can do that, you'll be amazed at how much charisma you'll suddenly have in the eyes of the media and public."

Hana didn't seem to have much fun being around Bruce Priklan, and I could understand why.

Bruce could, or would, not keep his hands off her for more than two seconds. He kept squeezing, patting, rubbing and otherwise touching her forearm, upper arm and neck—the parts of her where there was bare skin. He eyeballed her half-grown zoomers as she blushed fire-engine red. Bruce was so nonchalant about it, as if he were Uncle Brucie being affectionate with his favorite niece. Like fools, Lorna and I just looked away, sickened. This dirty old man was my age, and to Hana he may as well have been her grandfather, but did he give a shit? No chance; all he cared about was the boner in his pants and the jailbait who'd gotten him all worked up.

The fun was just beginning. Bruce had already ordered for us.

Our first course looked like an English muffin

stuffed with slimy spinach, all of it glistening under a generous topping of maple syrup. Bruce told us that this dish had a name, but I was too disgusted to listen.

"The chef here prepares things that are Asian with French influence, and vice versa," Bruce told us. "So I said, 'Show us what you can do.'"

I gestured to our server and handed the dish back to him. "Go run across the street and get me a Big Mac. If you can't do that, just bring me another Canadian Comfort over ice."

Hana Palmer guffawed as she picked at her food. Lorna tried to stifle a giggle. Lance said, "I don't care what this is, I'm starved." He tucked it all away.

"This next course," Bruce said, "will show you what a truly innovative chef our man in the kitchen truly is."

Our server brought out something that I recognized as squid, oysters, clams an anchovies in a weird stew. The room suddenly smelled like a gynecologist's office.

I took out a hundred-dollar bill and pressed it into our server's hand. "There is no way I'm going to eat that shit. Understand me? Take this money and run to McDonald's. Bring me back a Big Mac, fries and a Coke."

"Same for me," said Lorna, grimacing at the seafood stew in front of her.

"Make mine a Quarter Pounder with Cheese," said Hana Palmer, wiping away a tear. "No onions."

Throughout dinner, dessert and coffee, Bruce bored us all shitless with his talk about International Athletics Management. I got the feeling that Bruce wasn't sure where he ended and his agency began. Then I got the feeling that Bruce Priklans and IAM were one and the same.

Lance got up, yawning and stretching. Then he left.

Hana, seeing that Lance had the balls to split, got up and hustled out the door before Bruce could kiss her goodnight. She climbed into the limousine outside and went back to the Hyatt or Hilton or Doubletree at which all the network people were staying.

"Please stay and have another cup of coffee," Bruce said to Lorna and me.

"Any more coffee," she told him, "and I'll be up all night."

"Big day tomorrow," Bruce said.

"That's one of the reasons I'll be up all night," Lorna said.

"You've got money bet on both fighters in the ring," Bruce said. "You can't lose."

"So I'll be happy for one," she said, "and unhappy for the other."

"Wait a minute," I interjected. "You make it sound as if it's between Lance and me, period. There are a few other world-class players out there who could win this thing very easily. The leader chokes while the guy who's a few strokes back makes some big putts and ends up winning the whole thing. Happens all the time. It's called golf. I guess that's why so many people like it so much."

"I hate all the anxiety I'm feeling," Lorna said, lighting a cigarette.

"You're right, Grover," Bruce said. "It still is anyone's tournament, but it will *probably* be you or Lance who wins the thing. You or Lance. Him or you."

"Let's talk about something else," Lorna said.

"Great idea," said Bruce. "Grover, how much money do you think you would make by winning the tournament tomorrow?"

"The winner's purse is one-point-four million

dollars."

"Aside from that."

"Well, I would get the gratification that comes from finally winning a major. My fee for appearances would increase. I would be set financially for a very long time."

"How much would it be worth to Lance Priklan?" he asked.

"Tell me."

"Twenty million."

"No shit?" I muttered.

"And twenty mil is just the beginning. Wrap your brain around *that*."

"It won't fit. The number is too big or my brain is too small."

"Twenty fuckin' mil, Grover."

"I really, *really* don't like where this conversation is going," I told him.

"It's just talk. Bunch of words that don't mean shit."

I sighed, looked down, then around, and finally at him. I shook my head and tsked. "You are a son of a bitch, Pricklan."

He smiled. "I've been called worse names by better men."

"OK," Lorna said, "would someone please tell me what you two are talking about? I understand exactly none of it."

"Then let me fill you in," I said. "Bruce here has just suggested that, tomorrow, if it comes down to me versus Lance, it might be terrific if I let Lance win for the good of Bruce's talent agency."

Lorna glowered at Bruce. She shuddered. "Well…?"

"Just looking after my client," he said.

"Bruce," she said, "when you were playing college

football, if someone had offered you big money to fumble away the ball during the Rose Bowl, would you have said yes?"

"Apples and oranges, Lorna."

"Grover's right, Bruce. You *are* a son of a bitch, and if I wasn't such a lady, I would kick your balls up through the roof of your mouth." She turned to me. "Take me home *tout de suite*."

"You're the boss."

Outside, I said to her, "You know, of course, that you're no longer under consideration for that big job with IAM."

"Hold me while I cry," she retorted, rolling her eyes.

"I'm glad you did it. I was getting nauseated in there, watching Bruce feel up Hana."

"I don't think *she* liked it much, either."

"If you had gone to work for him, I don't think he would have let you do very much. Your job would have been to hang out at the office and look important while he made all the big decisions. Still, he would have made sure you were the most overcompensated worker around. Do you regret telling him off and losing out on that?"

"Fuck no," she said, and we both laughed.

54

Lance and I stood there waiting our turn to go in the final round. Countless fans stood behind the rope, staring at both of us—mostly Lance, because he was so handsome, but also at me, because it had come down to just the two of us. I figured I could make good shots on the holes ahead of us because they were straightforward enough. Later on, with the back nine, I knew I had to be careful. I hoped Lance's own cockiness and pulverizing strength would cause him to do a few stupid things and cost him the tournament.

Lance and I had already shaken hands and chuckled at each other to show all the spectators that we were both gentlemen and sportsmen who liked each other, and that the loser would not try to beat the shit out of the winner.

"Look at all the people and cameras," I said to him. "This is what it's all about, right? A couple of elite golfers competing against each other for the enjoyment of the masses."

He shrugged. "If you say so."

I turned to Everett. "The trophy they give the winner? It's big and heavy, but it has no inherent value. It's made of cheap shit. I guess the Oscars are like that, too—just symbols of creative achievement. They should be made of gold or something else precious."

He sighed. "Maybe you jes' better keep your mind golf right now 'stead of worryin' about gold Oscars and such."

If I had been much closer to Lance Priklan's age, I might have felt humiliated by watching him almost effortlessly drive the ball twice as far as I did on every hole, but I stood there, smug and grinning, because I knew that I had already forgotten more than he had ever learned. Plus, I was banging his mum.

We both made even pars on one hole after another. I hit mine with professional consistency and relentlessness, and Lance did his thing his way.

Check this out: One hole, over 500 yards, had a par-five. I made my best drive off the tee, landed in the middle of the fairway and made it onto the green with my next shot. Lance hauled off and pulverized his tee shot so that it sailed down the fairway and bounced onto the green. Fortunately, he wasn't the world's greatest putter, so we tied on that hole.

Some observers have said that Lance is the Mike Tyson of golf, with his huge hands and awesome strength.

I felt relieved that the other players on the leaderboard, who were playing right in front of us, weren't doing as well as we were. When the other guys play as well as I do, and the crowds cheer for them and mostly ignore me, leaving me disappointed and surly. This time, the big players started falling behind and soon it became clear that the winner would be me or Lance.

Players sometimes insist that they ignore the leaderboard while they have a chance of winning the tournament. If so, they're liars or imbeciles, or just there for the money, which to me makes them worse than liars or imbeciles.

I feel better, and play better, when I'm aware of

everything that's going on around me. It's when I'm ignorant and oblivious that I start to freak out.

Lance's physical strength hurt him on the ninth hole, a par-three that was remarkable only because it was a par-three.

The people who design golf courses don't build par-threes on the ninth any more. It just doesn't go well with the rest of the course. But those par-threes are fairly common on the older courses, where the designers did their best with the land they had to work with.

The length of the hole, two football fields, demanded that I tee off as hard as possible, while Lance just did his usual thing and hammered his ball. But then his ball just stayed up there, rising, rising. It went over the flag, over the green and, I thought for a moment, over the sun.

"Dammit!" he shouted.

"Gitcher ass back down here!" shouted his caddy.

We had two rules officials with us, who walked along with Lance and me. One of them, Spaz Haller, was the current president of the U.S. P.G.A. and the boss of some golf course near the Great Lakes. Our "walking observer," River Barnes, was the honcho at some country club in southern California. They ruled that Lance should get some relief in the form of having his ball placed one club length from the grandstand, which helped him not at all.

Lance wiped his face in frustration as he took out his club and hit the ball. A few strokes later, he finally got the ball into the cup for a double-bogey five.

I got very lucky and sank a 30-foot putt, which put me ahead of Lance and everyone else.

As we departed the ninth green and headed for the

10th, I remarked to Lance, "Hard luck on that one. You don't know your own strength sometimes."

He shook his head. "Plus, my putting sucks. Shitfuck!"

I'd looked around for Lorna from time to time but couldn't find her anywhere. "Lance, have you seen your mum anywhere?"

"I thought that was *your* job."

"Well, I guess it is."

We both made pars for the two holes on the back, then Lance made the 12th hole his bitch. I did my best on the 550-yarder and made par five, Lance swung his mighty shaft and reached the green on two strokes, then made birdie, bringing himself to within two strokes of me.

He stayed within two strokes of me, and we both parred the 13th and 14th holes. That's how it was when we got to the Freaky Four, Oakland Hills' last four holes that had given so much grief to so many golfers for so damn long.

Lance went first at the 15th. He gave his ball a mighty ride that sailed over a bunker in the middle of the fairway. He ended up with a simple pitch to enter the green on the 400-yard hole. Lance gave a simple nothin'-to-it shrug as he handed his driver back to his caddy.

For Lance, the long hit were easy; the lobs and putts fucked him up. He failed to make a birdie.

The 16th hole fucked up my brain.

Phil Mickelson had the best score of all the guys who had already finished, but I would beat him easily. No matter how much I didn't want to fight it out to the end with Lance Priklan, that's how it was: Just the two of us.

He teed up and hit another moonshot on the 16th, and his ball ended up just a short distance from the green.

I reached into my bag and took out my driver. "Think I should use this? I've done all right with it so far today."

He nodded. "If it makes you comfortable, use it."

Comfort didn't mean jackshit to me. I needed power. Fortunately, I had that, too.

Unfortunately, I hit it too hard, and too far to the right. I watched as my ball headed straight for the water. It is very difficult to describe such a feeling. A severe hangover is comparable.

The official at the scene gestured that my ball was in a hazard—between the water and a marked-off red line. My lie really wasn't that bad, and I wanted to hit my ball before I lost my nerve and gave in to despair.

Bad idea.

I did the dumbest thing I had ever done—except for marrying a couple of bitches who treated me like dog shit and took my money.

Afraid of hitting the ball too hard, I ended up hitting it too softly, and the clubface failed to strike the ball properly. The ball sailed right into the water.

I heard weird sounds from the gallery. The kind of sounds they usually don't direct at Grover Bobbitt.

Everett and I stood there for the longest time, just looking at each other. Neither of us could quite believe what we had just seen. Maybe he was thing, *Way to go, asshole. You just lost another major. Could you be an even bigger fuckup?*

Just then I heard Hana Palmer.

"Grover? Are you looking for your ball? It's over here."

She stood ten feet behind me, pointing at a ball.

"What the—"

"This is yours," she said. "I'm sure of it."

"I guess that one is mine, but I've just hit one into the water, so I'm over and done with, Hana."

She shook her head. "Not at all. There is no penalty for playing the wrong ball in a hazard."

"Oh, really?"

"Yes, *really*." Her face hardened a bit. "There is no penalty for playing the wrong ball in a hazard. I know about these things."

I turned to River Barnes, the official, and asked, "Is Hana right? I don't know the rules that well, and I've never been in this kind of situation before."

Hana nodded. "I'm sure I'm right—look it up."

"Thanks, I'll do that." Barnes took out his copy of the rule book and checked it out. After a few very long minutes, he closed the book, shook his head and looked at Hana, arching his eyebrows. "You got that one right, little girl," he said to the teenager who stood half a foot taller than himself. To me, he said, "Grover, looks like you can play this one with impunity."

With a thanks-a-million wink at Hana, who offered me a sure-no-problem smile in return, I grabbed my eight-iron and whacked my ball out onto the fairway before River Barnes could decide to take another look at his tattered black rule book.

Thanks to a 15-year-old child-woman, I had gone from being fucked in the ass again to just fine and dandy.

I was nearly a football field away from the green for my third shot. My next stroke got my ball within a few feet of the pin, and I tapped it in with no trouble. Lance kept up with me.

We both parred the 17th, too—I hit a grandmotherly tee shot but got the ball into the cup in three strokes, while Lance got onto the green on his drive from the tee but needed three putts to get his ball into the hole. I felt no shame or embarrassment over playing it safe by playing the final hole for a bogey five. I did it with a careful drive from the tee, a thoroughly unimpressive layup, then a pitch and a pair of putts from a dozen feet. It wasn't pretty, but it worked, and I took it.

I have always believed that the sweetest thing on God's green earth was a short putt to win a major tournament.

55

That moment, like all other remarkable ones in a person's life, is difficult for me to recall. I know that people were hugging me, hoisting me up into the air, patting me and cheering for me as if I'd just saved the world. Everett, Gil Donaldo, Jake Grimsley and a few others. Then Lorna broke through and thrust herself into my arms.

"Where the hell you been?" I shouted over the cheers and applause as she kissed my ear. "Couldn't find you all day."

I knew the fans would have made more noise if the big handsome stud had won. His mum and I barreled through the crowd and caught up with him. He shook my hand and forced a smile.

His mum and I took him into a sort of bear huge. "Lance," I said, "you're going to win a shitload of these things by the time you're my age. But this one's mine. OK?"

"I hear ya," he said, nodding. "You got a huge break on sixteen, but that four you made? Unreal. Outrageous."

I smiled.

Lorna said she wanted to go wash the day off her. She guessed that the media would want to keep me around a little while to answer questions and make comments.

"See you back at the hotel," she said. "Don't forget the trophy."

I went into the press center and gave them

something for dissemination. I felt more exhausted than elated.

The reporters asked me many questions about the ruling at the 16th. "I'd be happy to break off a bit of the trophy and give it to Hana," I said, and got a laugh.

They asked why I didn't know the rules of golf better.

"Well, at least I know them better than you guys do," I retorted. Then, "I guess at this level we put our energy into playing the game, not memorizing its rules. Unless the golfer's name is Hana Palmer."

A writer asked, "Grover, are you ashamed of your bogey-five on the final hole?"

"Nope. I'm not ashamed to say that I play golf intelligently." I added, "Maybe it would have been a better story for you if ol' Grover here had blown it again and Lance Priklan or Hana Palmer had won it on the final hole. Well, sorry. You're stuck with me this time."

I heard some applause as I entered the hotel lobby with the trophy in my arms and headed for the elevator. I smiled and nodded, feeling prouder than a man had a right to be.

I set the trophy on the table of our suite's living room and felt pleased to see an unopened bottle of Canadian Comfort with a bucket of ice and two glasses. I stood pouring myself a drink when Lorna emerged from the washroom after a long bath. She wore snug, faded Levi's and a red halter top.

"Hey, winner, I got my hair done and a massage to celebrate," she said.

"I'm sure you notice how intelligent I look now," I

told her. "I mean, I must look more intelligent than I did this morning. At least *I* think so. Now that I have all the intelligence that winning a major confers, I think my head is already getting bigger. I'm going to have to buy a larger golf cap."

"Grover?" Lorna said, putting her arms around me.

"Yes?" I said, putting my arms around her.

"Just don't get too smart," she said, grinning. "I'm pretty smart myself."